THE DARKEST
NIGHT

A MARKED SOULS CHRISTMAS NOVELLA

JESSA SLADE

Acknowledgments

My thanks to the marvelous author Delilah Marvelle for her priceless feedback. (To wit: "Schwing? Or no schwing?" Schwing, of course!)

Fervent thanks also to Mom ("This one seems a little more sacrilegious." Which part?) and Sis ("The hero is wearing a skirt?" No, shirt. Damn typos!) for fearlessly opening any email I send them.

As always, my deep love to Scott for the soup and support.

And to the Marked Souls readers, I can never thank you enough. I hope you enjoy The Darkest Night.

CHAPTER I

The nights before Christmas were annoying enough to make even an angel swear.

Cyril Fane forgave himself as he cursed and swerved his Porsche around a minivan of suburbanites gawking at the holiday lights strung along the Magnificent Mile. Not yet rush hour and already Chicago's downtown bustled with holiday crowds, filling the early darkness with their shopping bags, their good cheer, and their damnably low-horsepower vehicles. If they knew how the longer, darker nights provided ever-deeper shadows for the demonic tenebrae, they would all scuttle home.

Of course, not everyone had a home waiting for them.

Fane crushed the thought like a burned-out Christmas light bulb. Useless. But the warning from the afternoon visit with his only remaining friend in the sphericanum still scalded: *"...Lost your abraxas to the djinn-man... Conspiring with the talyan... Exiled... Don't come back, Fane, or we will slay you."*

With friends like that, who needed demons?

Swearing again, he cut over to Lake Shore Drive, aimed toward his big empty house, and punched the Porsche up to law-of-man breaking speeds. God would forgive even an ex-sphericanum warden like him.

Or not.

At the last exit, Fane changed his mind and circled into the city, past the high rises and towers, back toward the rougher neighborhoods. No twinkling lights here, just the fading blacklight glow of demon ichor, faintly visible to the angel within him, marking where the tenebrae had passed on their own nefarious tasks. Spits of icy rain caught the yellow, sodium-vapor glow from the street lights, as if the heavens were pissing on him.

The winter weather—if not the unseen demons—seemed to have scared off the crowds as he cruised past the Mortal Coil. The night club usually had a long line of hipsters, ravers and Goths straggling around the three-story brick building into the alley, where they did whatever hipsters, ravers and Goths did in alleys. But tonight, nothing, nobody.

Maybe the talyan had commandeered the place for a twelve-step meeting. The Chicago league of demon-possessed warriors often spent their afterhours in the crude and morally questionable environs of the night club. *Step whatever: Admit that a Higher Power has totally hosed us...*

He parked the Porsche directly under one of the street lights, said a skeptical prayer it would still be there when he returned, and headed for the door. For once, he might be able to appreciate a good bar fight.

The old bricks were rounded with age, but the stained glass in the circular window above the door glittered sharply. The snake eating its tail seemed to stare at him with ageless mockery in its one yellow eye. He ignored it and reached for the handle, but the curved wrought iron jerked out of his grasp.

In the darkened doorway, Bella gasped, one hand over her heart. "Jesus Christ."

"Not for a few more days," Fane said. "There's still time to shop."

She glared at him, almost as baleful as the snake above her. Behind her old-fashioned, cat's-eye glasses—out of place on her youthful face—her eyes were clouded, reflecting a blue-white smoke. Fane peered at her, wondering how much she could see through the cataracts. He'd heard a couple of the talyan wondering the same, and not just in the physical sense. The Mortal Coil's young mistress knew things sometimes, things most people couldn't fathom. The cataracts made her eyes look old when she couldn't be much past her mid-twenties.

Whether she saw or just sensed his perusal, she patted her red beehive self-consciously. "We're closed."

She must be able to see something, he decided. How else could she arrange such an elaborate hairstyle? The red locks were plumped high and smooth with only two curls wisping down on either side, and he guessed those mirrored runaways were probably deliberate. From what little he knew of Bella McGreay, she had too many secrets to let a stray hair be just a stray hair.

Without touching him even though he'd claimed a good chunk of the doorway in his double-breasted, black wool peacoat, she took a step forward. "Can't you read the sign?"

He leaned sideways, not willing to give up his space, to read the paper taped in the window. "'*Go home for the holidays, you fucking delinquents,*'" he read aloud. He tapped the glass. "The Santa hat on the skull and crossbones is a nice touch."

"Thank you. I was feeling festive. Good-bye, Warden Fane." She reached around him for the door handle, and the fake fur cuff of her coat grazed his hand.

A little spark of static electricity—not uncommon in the dry winter air—jumped between them. He frowned at the sting. "Ex-warden. I was hoping to find Liam and his crew here tonight."

She pointed one gloved finger toward the sign. "Closed. Go home. Remember?"

"I know they didn't go home to their families."

"No. Their cousins are on the prowl tonight, as every night." She lifted her face to the black sky. For a heartbeat, the yellow of the street lights flashed across her glasses. "They'll never go home."

Fane wasn't sure if 'they' meant the talyan or the tenebrae demons they hunted, but he supposed it didn't matter. The league talyan, possessed by repentant teshuva demons, were every bit as cast out as their decidedly unrepentant brethren.

As he was cast out.

He widened his stance, forcing her back a step if she didn't want to touch him. "Maybe I can leave them a message with you."

She scowled. "Just because I'm eloquent with pen and paper—"

"I'll be quick."

"Ever heard of the telephone?"

"This isn't the sort of message I want anyone else to hear." The talyan had evidence that the sphericanum, for all its divine calling, had a predilection for infiltrating more terrestrial calls. "Warrantless wiretapping seems to be all the rage these days."

Her scowl deepened. "Then go find them. They're out there, somewhere. Look in the dark corners."

"I doubt they want to see me again, considering my abraxas is empowering the enemy. As if almost getting the oldest known female talya and their Bookkeeper killed wasn't bad enough."

After a moment, she swept her hand inward. "Fine." Her long-suffering sigh wreathed the freezing air around her beehive. "Quick, though."

He stepped into the cavernous club and waited for his eyes to adjust. For all the winter darkness outside, inside was gloomier yet. Illuminated rope lights lined the bar at the far end of the room and one pendant light glowed over the cash register, but other than that, only the red glow of the exit signs lit the space. His breath puffed out—was it colder in here than out there?—and he pulled his coat tighter around him.

He followed the clack of the red heels on Bella's high-laced fake fur boots. The echo across the dance floor seemed louder than it needed to be, a rhythm of annoyance. He could relate.

At the counter, he paused while she went behind the bar. From beside the cash register, she pulled a kitchen ticket book and pen, and yanked off a page. "I can't promise I'll see them anytime soon," she warned. "They only come here after really bad nights."

"Then I imagine they'll be in here sooner rather than later."

She tilted her head as if studying him, or maybe just considering the nature of the threat behind his words. She took a breath, then let it out again in a swirl. "What do you want to tell them?"

"I met with a friend in the sphericanum today," he started.

"Dear Marked Souls," she muttered as she wrote. "Today I had a death wish…"

He couldn't help himself. He laughed. The sound came out like a ghost, white and drifting in the frigid air. "I figured I could risk the meeting since my friend would want to tell me off one last time. Nothing the sphericanum likes better than chastising."

"Charming fellow."

"She." Fane shrugged. "And at least she'd shoot me in the face, not in the back."

Bella poised the pen over the paper again. "Admires honesty in a woman above all. Has a sweet-ass ride. How about I write a personals ad for you instead?"

His amusement chilled. "I don't do personal."

"Christmas must be very lonely for you." She gave him a catty grin to match her glasses.

He gripped the edge of the bar. "I thought we were making this quick."

"By all means, go on."

He glowered. "Tell Liam the sphericanum has also noticed the change in tenebrae activity. Where we—they—were seeing an uptick in demonic energy, since Thorne took over—"

She tapped the pen against her lower lip. Like her beehive hair and her faux fur heels, her wide mouth was another shade of red too lush to be real. "Took your sword, you mean?"

So much for bee-stung lips. She *was* the stinger. He inhaled once, slow and deep, reaching for the peace that was his. Or *had been* his when his abraxas was in his hand. Of course, the peace had really been his only when he was chopping demons to pieces.

The cheap plastic of the counter creaked under his fingers. "Since Thorne, the sphericanum, like the talyan, have had fewer tenebrae encounters—"

"But that's good," she interrupted. "That's, like, the definition of good. No evil."

He shook his head and continued, "Fewer encounters even though the amount of ambient demonic energy has not decreased."

"So the horde hasn't gone anywhere. They are just..." She let out a shaky twist of breath.

"Waiting," he finished. "For something. Which can't be good. Why is it so damned cold in here?"

"Because it's almost the longest night of the year." She fell silent—miraculous, he thought, with unnecessary acidity—her head bowed. Then she tucked the pen behind her ear. "What's your poison?"

The abrupt zag of their conversation loosened his grip on the counter and his anger. "What?"

"A drink. It's what I do here." She stripped out of her heavy parka, revealing the vermillion-hued wrap dress underneath. "What do you like?"

The wrap's deep V neck revealed more of her cleavage than seemed necessary on a winter night when the bar was closed. His fingers itched to pull the V tight around her pale skin. "I don't drink."

"Ever?"

"Ever."

"Which explains why you're such a dried-up old sourpuss."

He yanked his attention away from where it had wandered. "Excuse me?"

"Oh. Did I say that aloud?"

"To my face."

"Well, I hear you like honesty in your women."

"I don't do *women* either," he said through gritted teeth. To be teased when he couldn't even remember the last time…

"I thought a lot of religions were anti-gay," she mused. "It's good to know that at least the sphericanum—"

"I'm not gay," he said.

"—accepts you," she went on blithely. "You should be so proud. Not flaming, sadly, not since you lost your sanctified sword—"

"Enough."

"How do you get consecrated weapons to be fiery, anyway? Is it, like, holy lighter fluid? I bet you were convenient to have around at all the blesséd barbecues." She accented the word just as the sphericaenum did, but with an added fillip of scorn. "I wish it was summer right now—"

He lunged across the bar and put his hand over her mouth. Against his palm, her lips were soft, yielding, very unlike her words. His bare skin tingled where he touched her, as if the static electricity had zapped him again.

Behind the cat's-eye glasses, her cloudy eyes widened.

"Just pour."

She nodded slowly. He pulled back his hand.

Her mouth was still that lush, unbelievable red, leaving not the barest smudge of lipstick across his skin. Maybe he'd been wrong to think she was all artifice. Certainly whatever she thought seemed to spill out of those lavish, red lips.

She washed her hands at the sink and turned to the wall of liquor behind the bar. On other nights, he'd seen the wall lit, light sticks on each shelf gleaming upward through the glass bottles, row upon row of smooth, flowing, jewel-toned sculptures celebrating wickedness and wantonness. Although it was all dark now, still Bella's hands went unerringly to each bottle.

Almost against his will, as if he'd already had too much to drink, he found his gaze tracing the shape of her through the wrap. The deep red was a ruse. Though it screamed for attention, underneath she was actually fine boned, tall only because of her ridiculous red boot heels, and almost fragile, like some retro Irish fairy. No wonder Liam Niall, the boss of the Chicago talyan, had gravitated to the Mortal Coil. With his own rough Irish history, he must have found some comfort—or at least familiarity—in the acerbic Bella McGreay.

For some reason, the thought of the tall, rangy league leader and the club's mistress made Fane's hackles prickle. He reminded himself Niall had found the love of his warrior life when he hooked up with the spunky Jilly Chan. The symballein bond linking male and female talyan had only been legend—even the sphericanum's ancient records had forgotten when the bond was truth—but in his short, unwilling time with the Chicago talyan, Fane had seen legend come to life.

What a miracle for the demon-ridden man, to find someone whose soul—flaws and all—perfectly aligned with his own...

Over her shoulder, Bella asked, "Why don't you drink?"

Distracted by his own thoughts, Fane answered a touch too honestly, "Because for a time I was doing too much of it."

She turned, a tumbler and a shot glass in one hand, an unlabeled bottle in the other. The tumbler was cupped under her palm, the shot glass full of some dark liquid pinched with her finger inside the rim. She set the glasses on the counter and pushed the tumbler toward him, then downed the shot and licked her fingertip. "So why are you drinking now?"

He looked away from her dampened finger. "Because recently I haven't been doing it enough." And he'd come to rely too heavily on the temptation-blunting effect of his lost abraxas if the mere glimpse of her tongue made him this edgy.

She filled her glass again, all the way to the rim this time. "I hear you. The talyan have been in here almost every night, bitching and drinking. First Corvus Valerius and that solvo drug turning people into soulless zombies and then soul bombs breaking open portals into hell. Now Thorne Halfmoon. God knows what he'll do."

"God might know, but He hasn't shared any info with the sphericanum."

She lifted her glass. "Maybe the devil will tell."

He clinked his glass against hers. "Here's hoping."

Suddenly reckless, he tossed back half the tumbler. The bite and rush of whiskey sour heat made him gasp. He idly noted he couldn't see his cold breath anymore. Although if someone lit a match...

Bella lifted one brow. "Like it? The whisky's a single cask from a local distiller, with a little secret of my own."

"Fire and brimstone?"

She laughed, although the sound was almost hollow. "Something like that." She poured a third shot but just held it.

The warmth drifted down through his belly, and he studied her more closely while taking a wary sip. "So what's your deal, Bella?"

She made another soft noise, one he couldn't identify. "No deals. Actually, I was thinking about charging you."

From his wallet, he thumbed out a bill—a big one, although he didn't check to see how big—and pushed it across the counter. "For your troubles."

She touched the corner of the paper. "Worse troubles ahead."

He reached for his wallet again, but she just repeated that empty laugh. "Does that always get you out of trouble?"

"No. I used to chop off heads too."

She pocketed the cash. "Ah, a multi-disciplinary approach. You didn't learn that from the sphericanum."

He gave her a reproving look. "You must have learned that cynicism from the talyan."

She tipped one shoulder in a careless way that made the red V neckline buckle around her breasts. "I don't think they'd appreciate your judgmental tone."

"The demon-ridden never do." He drank again to drown the errant notice of her breasts.

She matched his reckless motion, and when they thumped their empty glasses down at the same time, their knuckles brushed.

No static charge this time, thankfully, because he thought the slow burn of alcohol in his blood might have burst into flame if there'd been even one stray spark.

Hell, just standing near the red-on-red mystery girl kindled his senses. The loss of his abraxas' moderating influence was bad enough, but maybe his losses before were more to blame. It had been so long since he felt this…tempted. No wonder the talyan with their inner demons—repentant demons, but demons nonetheless—felt at home at the Mortal Coil.

She gave her empty shot glass a spin. "Can I get you something more, ex-warden Fane?"

His gaze fixed on her mouth as she said his name, the quick bite of her lip, the flick of her tongue against the back of her teeth. Since when did his name look like a sin?

With difficulty, he focused. "Nothing. I should be going."

But he didn't move. Not even when she boosted her elbows up onto the bar, leaned across the counter, and kissed him.

Chapter 2

She didn't have much time, so Bella brought out the big guns: open mouth, tongue, moan.

Thank God—well, thank the devil; no, thank her own damn self—for the little secret she'd added to his drink. Despite that crack about judgment, his judgment would be just enough impaired, or so she hoped, to make this easy. To make *him* easy. He might have a divine entity sharing his skin, but he was a man first, alone, on his way to being drunk. Even the sphericanum couldn't blame him.

Well, they probably would, but he wasn't with them anymore.

For tonight, he'd be with her.

Fane had come to the Mortal Coil only a few times before, meeting in back corners with the league warriors. Even without the talyan grumbling afterward, she would have known him for an angel-man. There was a light to him—not an easiness or happiness or flimsiness; not that sort of light, not any sort of obvious glow at all. But the divine entity had marked him, indelibly and invisibly, like the club's doorman stamped wrists with an ouroboros that shone only under a blacklight.

In the past, she had ignored him, all her instincts warning her she did not want that searching light turned on her. But tonight, the dark and the cold pressed down hard all around, a threat no one else could see, so she fought back with the soft, vibrant heat of his mouth on hers. If she could just stoke his light a little higher, just for tonight…

His hand came up to cup her jaw, his thumb at the point of her chin. She wriggled up higher onto the bar, faintly aware of the crash of glasses he swept aside. She would have laughed—or maybe yelled at him; glassware wasn't exactly cheap—but with his thumb, he forced her mouth wider and deepened the kiss.

Oh, he was so deep in her, his hand sliding behind her nape and tightening, tightening. Her heartbeat slammed through her, pushing the dark alcohol to her extremities, setting every nerve ending ablaze, and settling into her core where she felt the cold, hard knot melting, her sex unfurling like a slow out-of-season bloom. His whiskey perfume swirled around her, and she moaned again—helplessly and without artifice this time—around the wet tangle of their tongues.

His fingers tangled in her hair, triggering the inevitable collapse. He gripped the mass, and she arched her neck at the ruthless pleasure.

Then he yanked back, ripping her mouth away.

She gasped, not in pleasure this time.

"Bella." His growl roused something darker in her, and she clamped her hand over his, buried in her hair.

"You're hurting me." She thought her whimper would make his fingers spring open, but under her hand, his fist tightened.

"And you are…" He was still so close his hot, harsh breath scalded her bruised lips. "I don't know what you're doing."

She swallowed against the flutter of panic in her throat. Ex-warden he might be, but it was the sphericanum, not the man, who had her in his grip now. "It's called kissing."

"You're lying to me."

"No, really. It's called kissing. For a second there, you seemed to get the concept."

He released her, too quickly, almost shoving her away. She caught herself, sprawled awkwardly across the bar, and straightened her glasses on her nose. The other glasses were broken on the floor somewhere.

"Just say no," she murmured.

He slammed his open palm on the bar. The counter reverberated under her hands as she eased down to her feet.

"What do you want?" he demanded.

"I think you can figure that out." Shattered glass crunched under her heels. "I wasn't exactly hiding anything." Not about that, anyway.

"Are you working for Thorne?" From the ring of demand in his tone, she wondered if anyone had ever refused him.

This time she did laugh, loudly. "You really are clueless. Sorry about the kiss then."

He muttered something under his breath, something inappropriate for an angelic warden. Even an ex one. "Why are you tempting me?"

She waved one hand in irritation. "Don't make it all biblical." Did it even count as tempting if he resisted so easily? "You don't represent the sphericanum anymore."

"The talyan don't know what to make of you either."

"They shouldn't be so suspicious. I help them how I can."

"They need more."

"Don't we all?" She crouched to sweep up the glass.

Angelic-possessed humans didn't have wings, but Fane might as well have flown so quickly and quietly did he arrive behind the bar. He knelt beside her, his big body nudging her aside.

"Let me do it. You're going to cut yourself."

When was the last time someone had helped her pick up the pieces of anything? She steeled herself against any perilous weakening in her defenses. "What do you care? You just accused me of cahooting with a djinn-man." She didn't want to care that he cared, and yet...

"I don't want your blood on my hands." He managed to make it sound like it'd be such an inconvenience.

"It would be on *my* hands," she pointed out. "And anyway, you have enough on your hands you wouldn't notice a little more."

He paused on an indrawn breath, then he let it out slowly as he piled the glass in his palm with precise little clinks. "It was for a good cause, the cause of good."

Why the hesitation? Did he regret the demons he'd slain? Or just regret he wasn't still wielding his flaming sword of retribution? "Whatever," she grumbled to herself as she stood over him.

While he finished sweeping up the glass, the warmth of his him seeped into her legs, skin bared between the hem of her skirt and the top of her boots. In the same way he nudged her back with his body, his very presence edged out the cold and dark.

He dumped the broken glass into the trash can beside the register and washed his hands. The lemony scent of soap cleared some of the lingering boozy air.

"Thanks for cleaning up," she said stiffly. "I'll give your message to the talyan when I see them."

"Bella—"

"I wish you'd stop saying that."

"It's your name, isn't it?"

"You always say it like a warning or an accusation."

He ran one hand over his face, muffling his apology, such as it was. "That's the warden in me."

"Ex-warden," she retorted, then winced. What was the point of poking him with the reminder?

He leaned in. "Ex." His breath was a warm whisper against her cheek.

She startled a little, not realizing he'd come so close. "You can go now." As she angled her face to track him, her tone lifted too, so the words came out as if she was uncertain, more a question, like she wanted him to stay. *Oh, please stay.*

"Bella." This time, his voice held neither threat nor blame, but still some rough undercurrent, as if he were struggling across a tricky path. "You shocked me. A couple of times, actually."

"I would've thought you'd seen everything."

"Too much maybe, but not everything." He cracked his knuckles as if his empty hands made him edgy. "I hadn't made it that far up in the sphericanum."

And now he never would, not without his sword. The unspoken words hung between them.

"There is light in you still," she said. The divine presence didn't just evaporate. He would have the angel inside him until he died, even if the terrestrial organization of the sphericanum had no more use for him. She was suddenly, fiercely glad they had lost him, which meant she could find him. That lost light was the part she wanted, needed, as the city spun toward its darkest night. *Please stay, and lend me your light until the dawn.*

She took a hesitant step closer, so the fuzzy cuffs of her boots brushed his trousers. The exposed skin of her thighs—just a few inches, but how much more she wanted, needed—heated at his nearness.

"Cyril," she murmured and lifted her hand.

He caught her wrist, and for a breathless moment, she thought he would push her away again, but then he brought her fingertips to his face.

She traced the hard edges of his jaw and cheekbone, felt the flex of muscle as he swallowed. She touched his lower lip. Almost as hard. An unyielding man. Or was that the angel in him? What other parts of him would be as hard? The want and need welled up, more violently now, weakening her bare knees, and she swayed toward him.

He anchored one hand at the small of her back and reeled her into his chest.

This time, she had no opportunity to power up her arsenal. His mouth slanted across hers with ferocious intent, stealing her breath. She leaned into him, giving it up, willing to give more, so much more. Not everything, of course. Some parts he couldn't be allowed to see, no one must see.

But the good parts… She loosened the wrap of her dress and let the V gape to her navel.

Fane dragged his mouth free. His hands went to the edges of the V, eased it wider. "Ah, just looking at you makes me hot." His voice was an even rougher growl than before, as if his path had not appreciably smoothed but he was determined to find his way.

Frigid air whispered across her bared skin, and she shivered.

"But you're cold," he murmured.

"I don't even feel it," she said honestly.

"Let me make sure of that." He kissed his way down her throat to her collarbone, then lower, over the swell of her breast filling the demi-cup of her bra. "It's all you in here." He brushed his lips over her swelling flesh. "I wondered how it could be. You are so…"

She waited a moment for him to finish, then suggested, "Bosomy?"

"So beautiful," he whispered against her skin, still moving down, loosening the wrap with every inch he uncovered. He knelt at her feet. "I can't believe you…"

No, he couldn't, but she didn't want him to go there. "Angels have to believe," she reminded him. "Job requirement."

"They fired me," he pointed out.

"Use that fire for good."

He circled his tongue around her navel and she gasped. She braced her hands on his shoulders as the dress fell open, exposing her to his gaze, his hands, his tongue.

He kissed a line across the top of her panties, his hot breath seeming to infuse the silky fabric, an advance army stealing between her legs. When he tangled his fingers in the fabric over her hips, twisting it tighter, she whimpered at the echoing pull across her sex. His soft laugh sent another flare of heat over her skin, as he slicked his hands down the backs of her thighs, drawing the panties down too, urging her legs apart. But when she complied, he grasped her hips and with one strong boost, rose to his feet, lifting her to the bar counter. He leaned his hips between her spread thighs and kissed her again, his tongue a hot and heavy portent of more to come.

She tore her mouth away and flexed her fingers on his shoulders, digging for the bulk of muscle beneath the heavy wool of his coat. "Take this off. I want to feel you."

Without moving from between her thighs, he wrenched off the coat while her fingers made quick work of the buttons she found centered down his chest. She groaned when she found the T-shirt underneath.

He chuckled, at least until she grasped the collar and ripped the T-shirt wide open. "Hey now!"

"I've shocked you again," she guessed. "The trick with tearing a T-shirt, as with most things in life, is not to hesitate. You gotta go all in." She leaned forward and pressed her lips to the notch of his throat. "All the way in."

Under her kiss, his pulse leaped. She walked her hands down his chest, exploring the faint sprinkling of hair across his pecs that trailed away to nothing until she hooked her fingers into the waist of his trousers and her fingertips brushed his crisp pubic curls.

His hips jerked. "I want…"

"Me too," she promised.

With a strangled curse, he jerked her closer to the edge of the counter, so her body was flush against his, bare skin to bare skin, their hearts thudding against each other, finding one beat. She speared her fingers through the thick, soft wave of his hair and angled her mouth under his for one last, deep kiss, the kind they called soul kissing.

She certainly hoped not.

She broke free and skimmed her hands down his arms, shedding his shirt and remnants of his T-shirt. The button and zipper of his trousers were harder since he was standing so close, but she pushed down the material to bunch at his hips. His cock thrust toward her, hotter than anything in the bar, so hot she almost imagined a glow. Just let the cold dark try to get her now. She had an angel between her thighs.

"Bella," he said again.

"No warnings," she said.

"But I didn't bring—"

She kicked her booted foot across the space between the bar and the back counter, and her heel caught the cash register. It sprang open, bell pealing. "There."

Fane coughed. "You keep your condoms in the cash register?"

"The money shot."

He strained backward to reach without leaving her, and the foil crinkled in his hand. He paused. "These are old."

"Is that the angelic way of saying thank you for not being a slut?" She flexed her legs, urging him closer.

"Exactly one year old."

She didn't like the look of calculation on his face. Time had never been her friend. "My Christmas fuck."

"You have such a mouth." He kissed her again, hard, his strong arms braced on either side of her so she felt like he was consuming her from every direction.

She whimpered as the fever of him worked deeper. She coiled her legs behind his hips and drew him in.

"Wait," he said breathlessly. "I have to—"

"Let me." She snatched the open condom wrapper from his grip and sheathed him. His flesh surged in her hand. "Now, Cyril."

"But—"

She strained toward him. "Talk later." She might not have a later if she didn't have him now.

Still he lingered, his fingers finding the needy bud of her clit and giving her a soft caress. Without her breath, the noise from her mouth was barely a whine—this was no time for games—but that only seemed to embolden him. He stroked her again, still maddeningly gentle when she needed his light as high and bright and fierce as an explosion.

She lowered her hand between their bodies and gripped his sac. His balls tightened; pleasure or fear she didn't care. "Cyril, damn it—"

"Don't remind me."

For half a heartbeat, she wanted to reassure him. Exile from the sphericanum didn't equal damnation. It took more than that. She ought to know. But if she told him as much, he would question her and where would that get them?

"Stop thinking, angel-boy." She gave his balls a squeeze and then a flick of her finger along his crease. He bucked against her hips, she angled just so, and—ah!—finally, he was in her, his flesh sheathed in her, their breath and pulses ratcheting higher. She gasped at the possession, complete and carnal and oh-so human.

He wasn't huge—angelic possession didn't grant everlasting life or superpowers, in bed or anywhere else—but the hard, hot length of him stretched her tight passage with a pressure almost like pain, a reminder she was here, now, pinned to this bar by his cock and his whiskey-drenched mouth. She closed her eyes even as she opened her legs wider to the intimate invasion.

They couldn't come for her, not when she was coming.

He hauled her hips toward him, so her ass hung precariously on the edge of the bar, and she propped her heels on the narrow well. He bent her back, one hand under her breast to plump her nipple over the demi-cup bra. His mouth fastened on the aching tight peak, and the lightning pleasure shot all the way to her clit. She rocked against his pounding flesh, finding a rhythm that would have put her club's dance remixes to shame, and let his harsh breath in her ear drown out the whisper of winter she heard all around.

She curled over him, her hair tickling her breast and belly, her core tightening, tightening. "Cyril…"

He straightened with one more hard thrust of his cock deep inside and his tongue in her mouth. His big hand was hot over her crotch, and he stroked her clit with a deft thumb. Three… two… one… ignition.

She went off like a bottle rocket, from sizzling fuse to screaming launch. He laughed against her mouth and let her shriek while he pummeled her.

The throb of her orgasm matched his beat, unabated, and he groaned. "You feel so damned good. I can't…"

Three-two-never-mind-one-go, and he shouted aloud—some wordless, profane invocation—and convulsed against her. With a last gasp, she came again around his climax. She wasn't a sparkler, she was a whole multi-stage rocket with extra boosters. The black was all around her and she didn't give a damn because the light and heat and boom of him held it all at bay.

She slumped back on the bar, her head hanging off the far end, blood rushing to her brain as he stroked a few more times, with a deep groan, then pushed again, far inside. The thick pulse of him heated her from within, and she wanted to hold him there forever.

But slowly he withdrew, his finger brushing softly against her twitching clit. She gasped but didn't straighten.

She heard the wet squeal-snap of the condom coming off and the surprisingly loud plunk as it hit the garbage can. Man, how much had he come? Apparently she wasn't the only one going Methuselian lengths of time between carnal encounters.

She flinched in surprise as soft cotton tucked between her legs. He'd found the stack of bar rags under the counter.

"Sorry," he murmured. He kissed her navel, and she couldn't stop herself from running her fingers through his hair again. The thick strands sculpted themselves into waves under her petting hand like demanding cats.

She opened her eyes, not that it mattered. "What color?"

"Pink. Pink and cherry red. Like a dessert."

"You have pink hair?"

"What? No. I have brown hair, light brown. I thought you meant…" He kissed her again, much lower this time.

She jackknifed upright, stiff-arming him. "Whoa."

"Now I've shocked you." He sounded smug. "We'll save it for next time."

Next time? She reached for the edge of her wrap and pulled it around her to cinch the waist. If only her hair came together as easily. "That's an angel for ya. Always going for the save."

He swung her down off the counter, steadying her while her still-wobbly knees aligned with her boot heels. "Have you had dinner yet?"

First next time? Now dinner? "I was actually headed out for the night. I have some errands…"

"Oh." The smug note was gone from his voice.

She bit her tongue against the urge to explain more. They'd swapped body fluids, some fluids anyway, but that didn't mean they could share everything. In fact, now that her desperation had eased, she could see—despite being semi-sorta blind—how fucking an angel-man might just be her dumbest move in a lifetime of bad choices.

Still, biting her tongue made her taste the lingering flavor of whiskey, and her knees wobbled again. "I really should get going."

"Yeah, I was heading home, like the sign on your door said."

"Okay, that's good." And angel-men *were* good. Too good for the likes of her. "I'll see you around then." Except she wouldn't, really, what with her cataracts and all. She didn't even *want* to see him again.

"Yeah, right." His tone said he'd thought exactly the same thing. Just as well the clouded haze over her eyes shaded her from the worst of his angelic glare.

He helped her on with her coat and waited at the front door while she locked up. She wished he would just get in his fancy car and go.

But he lingered. "I was wondering if my car would still be here." He sounded a little disappointed, as if he wanted an excuse to stay. "Can I drop you off somewhere?"

"No, thanks. I get around fine." She prickled a little. Let him think she took pride in her independence. Independent sounded better than lonely. "I don't need a Porsche."

"How do you know what I drive?"

"Some of the talyan were complaining to me about their vehicular crap. They were wondering how much blacker they'd stain their souls if they rolled you for the Porsche."

"So you saved me."

"Actually, I told them a dozen Hail Marys and a few dead djinn-men would absolve them. I try to stay on their good sides."

He snorted. "I'll have to watch my back then."

A faint stir of guilt made her shift on her heels—or maybe that was just the last quiver of her orgasm—but she felt compelled to add, "You should find somebody to help you watch behind you, ex-Warden Fane. This is a bad time to be alone."

"Yeah. See you, Bella."

And when he said her name this time, it sounded like a threat and a promise in one.

CHAPTER 3

Bella waited for the rumble of the Porsche to fade before she ducked back down the alley to retrieve her car.

Nothing so nice as the Porsche, of course, but the club's generic little hatchback was respectably efficient for her employees to do whatever needed to be done around the place. Enough people used it that nobody wondered why sometimes the gas tank ran a little low. Anyway, it was her damn car, she could drive it whenever she wanted.

Even if the view was a little hazy.

With the night wearing on, there wouldn't be anyone where she was going. The whole point was no one would see her, so it didn't matter she couldn't quite see them.

She circled her chosen route quickly, just in case anyone was watching. This was the fourth year she'd done it, and so she'd had to hit some places for the second time. She'd made the afternoon news last year, and she didn't want to be prime time this year. She squelched the guilty feeling. Another side effect from being near an angel.

On her way back to the club, she passed through a familiar neighborhood, and curiosity nipped sharper than the guilt. Well, that wasn't such a terrible thing. Curiosity had never hurt anyone.

She touched the curved rim of her cat's-eye glasses wryly.

The nursing home where she pulled up was decorated for the season with a small herd of white-lighted reindeer, an umbrella-style fake Christmas tree, an inflatable menorah, and a large nativity scene with the plastic wise men draped in kente cloth colorful enough to burn through even the haziest cataracts.

"How inclusive," she murmured.

Too bad they'd never have room at the inn for traditions like hers.

She parked around the corner and headed up the sidewalk, heels crunching on the thick layer of salt pellets laid, no doubt, in preparation for the storm warnings that had been playing between the Christmas carols as she drove. The lake effect weather was almost as punishing as an angel.

Although the ache between her legs said punishment didn't have to be a bad thing.

What a thought to be having on the steps of a nursing home. Santa would definitely be putting her on the naughty list.

She had to be rung into the facility—this wasn't the time of year for residents to go wandering—but she wasn't surprised to hear the welcoming voice as the door opened.

"Bella? Hello. What are you doing out on a night like tonight?"

"Hi, Nanette." Bella had known the angelic-possessed woman would be working the holidays. Of course she would. After her husband had been murdered—collateral damage in the war between the talyan and impenitent djinn-men—Nanette had thrown herself into all sorts of charity work, as if she had something to atone for. Bella had heard through the talyan that Nanette volunteered at the nursing home; they'd steered her that way to keep an eye on her because they blamed themselves as much as Bella did and they knew better than the angel-possessed woman how atonement might never end.

Bella tilted her head, taking in the rumble of the TV—*It's a Wonderful Life* from the overwrought sound of it—and the scent of apple cider. She held out the gift in her hand. "I was in the neighborhood and thought I'd bring you and your residents some cookies."

"You made cookies for us? How sweet."

As Nanette relieved her of the small burden, Bella saw no reason to correct either of the woman's two mistaken statements.

She followed the soft squeak of Nanette's shoes. "How are you getting along?"

"Good." The squeaks stopped. "Okay. Better than before."

Bella pursed her lips. "You are a terrible liar."

Nanette sighed. "Even you can tell? Wait, I'm sorry, that was so rude. I didn't used to be rude."

"Blame the talyan."

"Oh, I do." Nanette's voice was softer than her shoes and very faintly bitter. "And myself, of course."

Bella swallowed. "Now it's my turn to be sorry."

"Don't be. You brought cookies. Now what else brought you here?" Nanette thumped her hand. "Have a seat."

Bella settled into the overstuffed chair. A whiff of old-person smell wreathed her for a moment, and she closed her eyes. Would she ever get to be old?

"I had a visit from Cyril Fane." She lowered her voice. "He wanted me to get a message to the talyan. I was surprised he didn't come to you."

"I don't see him or the talyan if I can help it," Nanette said. "Only Sera Littlejohn, since her father lives here. But if you need me to help—"

"I'll find them at the Coil soon enough." Bella paused. "But I was wondering about Fane..." To her surprise, her voice trailed off.

"Are you blushing?"

"Blushing? No. It's just hot in here." She smoothed the faux fur hem of her parka. She couldn't very well open it since she wasn't sure what incriminating evidence might be on her dress. "It just seemed strange he would come to me." Much less come inside her, although she was thankful he'd proven inclined to temptation.

"Not so strange, since I haven't been around to take his messages." Nanette's tone turned sly, or at least as sly as an angelic possessed could manage. "And not strange he'd find you. Mr. Fane likes nice things."

"Nice?" Bella infused the word with all her disbelief.

"Well, beautiful things," Nanette amended, as if even when she was being sly she couldn't stop herself from being honest.

Bella shook her head. "I just don't want to get caught in the middle of some sphericanum versus talyan silliness."

"Almost as bad, in its way, as the tenebraeternum." A dark note of mourning colored the angel-woman's voice. "The host and the league should both know better. The tenebrae demons are just evil."

Bella's throat tightened. "So true."

"But Mr. Fane is a good man. Angels are, of course, but the man is good too. Strict and stern, sometimes, and uncompromising on occasion, and maybe a little humorless…"

Bella remembered the sound of his laughter as she climaxed. "Where is the good part?"

"I'm getting there. Just wait a second… He has pretty blue eyes. Celestial even."

"No wonder I couldn't turn him away."

"Turn him away from what?"

Bella's cheeks burned again. "I mean I couldn't say no to passing his message along."

"Little messenger girl," Nanette said. "Like the angel at Christmas, bringing words to the waiting."

Not like that at all.

She stayed a little longer when Nanette asked if she'd be willing to walk through the halls. "Some of our residents don't have many visitors, and, well, sometimes if they see someone, they can tell themselves it's family."

Bella agreed, but only because she was amused an angelic possessed would be so adept with this lie. Maybe that's why it was called a white lie.

Most of the residents were more interested in the angel on the TV than the one in their midst, but they all had coos for Nanette and a few "hello, dears" for Bella.

"Such lovely hair," said one of the old ladies. "Pretty as a poinsettia."

Bella touched the ridiculously wayward mass. "Thank you, ma'am."

From behind her came a gruff scolding. "Tempting the devil. More devils every day."

"Pastor Littlejohn," Nanette said reprovingly. "We don't talk that way here."

"I'll talk as I like. I preached it for forty years. If I don't keep an eye out for the devil, who will?"

Bella angled her face, tracking the age-roughened voice. "Maybe it's time to let someone else take up the fight."

"Who? I thought I knew everything before, but I didn't know what to look for. Now I do." His voice rose, taking on the cadences of the pulpit. "They are in the shadows when we look away. They are in the darkness and the freezing cold. They are in us!"

Nanette shushed him. "There are no demons here. And it's winter in Chicago, so of course it's cold and dark."

The pastor's tone sharpened. "You are too innocent to see them, but I see them all around—"

Bella interrupted his tirade. "The demons should be home for the holidays, shouldn't they? They could be roasting their chestnuts in hellfire and singing carols backward."

Nanette coughed.

After a moment, the old man grunted. "You watch yourself, missy. Nothing a demon likes more than a disbeliever."

"So I've heard. Just keep watching, Pastor."

Nanette urged her away. "Sera visits every week, but she can't let him see her or he screams for hours. We don't know if it's his preaching or his dementia, but he sees the teshuva demon threaded through her soul."

"He doesn't see the demon. He sees the reflection of it in her eyes. Tell her to wear polarizing sunglasses when she's with him and they'll be fine."

Nanette's footsteps stopped, then pattered to catch up as Bella moved toward the front door. "Really? I've never heard such a thing. How did you know?"

Bella shrugged. "I've screamed once or twice myself."

Nanette buzzed her out after offering to call a cab, which Bella graciously and without further explanation refused. The angel-woman followed her out onto the porch. "Sera said she'd be coming by for Christmas. I'll tell her to bring sunglasses for her and Archer. And I'll let her know you wanted to speak with her."

That hadn't exactly been what she'd said, Bella reflected. The female talya who had been a thanatologist specializing in modern death rituals had an unusually—and uncomfortably—perceptive eye, sunglasses or no. But she thanked the angel-woman and made her way down the crunchy sidewalk.

"Happy Holidays," Nanette called.

Bella waved and kept walking.

But at the closing click of the door behind her, she stopped. Then she turned a right angle and prowled into the yard.

A porch rambling the front length of the building, festooned with plastic garland and icicle lights, had lots of nooks and crannies, and the obstacle course of holiday-themed statuary offered extra hiding places. But Bella sensed nothing amiss besides the eyesore of décor. Something was keeping Pastor Littlejohn on edge, but what could one old man discern that would have escaped Nanette with her angel and Sera with her repentant teshuva demon?

With a shake of her head, Bella aimed for the sidewalk again. As she passed the nativity scene, she snagged the illuminated infant out of the plastic hay. The cord snapped free and the light went out. The visible light anyway.

She tucked him under her arm and returned to her car where she tossed him into the trunk with a dozen other statues from her earlier stops. One of the more secular minded churches had even had its cookies for Santa out already, which would now bring more joy to the nursing home residents than the inevitable rats. Bella figured she was doing everyone a favor, though she doubted anyone else would see it that way.

Then again, no one on earth saw the way she did. Maybe she'd carelessly forgotten for a few moments in an angel-man's arms, but she wouldn't make that mistake again. She had another savior now. She'd found Jesus. A whole lotta Jesuses.

CHAPTER 4

Fane steered the Porsche through the darkness of the industrial district, watching the passing streetlights as if they might reveal answers to some of the dimness in his own head.

He'd brooded for only a couple of days, possibly a new record for him. Maybe it was the Christmas spirit.

He had to admit, being with Bella had knocked something loose. Something besides his morals. The way she'd taken what she wanted had reminded him, if he was cut off from the sphericanum, he had to take matters into his own hands. Which he should have done before but he'd been brooding.

At this time of night, the warehouses were abandoned, everyone gone for the night and maybe trying to sneak in a few extra days of vacation. Light gleamed from only one building, sullenly low and striped with black from the security bars, but light. He parked outside the @1 headquarters and went to the door.

The glass was smoked so he couldn't see inside, but he pushed the intercom button and waited. And waited. Then he pushed it again and held it down.

"I know you can see me," he said.

After a moment, a grumpy voice answered. "You're right. That's why I didn't answer."

"Let me in."

"I can't think of a single reason..." There was a muffled discussion of multiple voices. "Oh fine."

The door buzzed, and Fane pushed inside.

The foyer, which would have been a front desk area for a real business, was empty except for the steel buttresses reinforcing the walls and ceiling. It looked like a combination cathedral and apocalyptic bunker. Which, Fane figured, it basically was.

To his disgust, the angel inside him eased, the prickles that often marched his skin relaxed. He'd always wondered what kind of divine entity willingly left heaven to inhabit a human host. Was unending war against evil so enticing? Or maybe his angel hadn't left willingly. Maybe that's why it seemed to find a strange comfort amid the talyan.

Though he'd ever let them know that.

He stood staring up at the steel beams, lost in the darkness at the ceiling, until the thud of boots interrupted him.

Since the talyan were capable of absolute silence—even the females who occasionally chose stilettos—he knew the stomping was for his benefit.

He didn't look down. "You got my message?"

"We did. So why are you here?"

Fane finally straightened. "How's it going, Jonah?"

The talya crossed his arms over his chest. Well, he crossed one arm. The other arm was missing from the elbow down and had been replaced by a wicked hook. Talyan carried a mean grudge, and Fane had been instrumental in tricking Jonah's soul mate into taking on Corvus Valerius in the final fight of his evil life. "We didn't really need the sphericanum to confirm what we already knew."

Fane steepled his fingers—a cheap shot since he still had both his hands even if he didn't have his sword—but a pointed reminder of who held the high ground here. "I thought it was important the tenebrae energy in this city is either dissipating or being diverted."

"We don't deserve a holiday?"

"Wouldn't know. We've never gotten one."

After a moment, Jonah inclined his head. "Nanette talked to Sera yesterday. If the tenebrae are undergoing some sort of transformation, we'll figure it out."

"And you don't need my help," Fane finished.

"Didn't I say that? I'm pretty sure I implied it." The talya flexed his biceps.

Obviously the angel's comfort in the place was a direct reflection of the teshuva's willingness to accept it. Or maybe, once again, the difference between men and their preternatural symbionts was too vast to be overcome.

Still, he'd come here to make the effort.

"I want my sword back," he said.

"We don't have it. Thorne does. We have only a few shards left of the ancient abraxas extracted from Alyce. Certainly not enough to forge a new sword."

Fane lifted one brow. He hadn't brought up forging anything. Which made him wonder what exactly Liam Niall, with his background as a blacksmith in Ireland, was doing with the remains of the ambraxas. "I don't want a new sword. I want mine."

"Then I guess you shouldn't have lost it."

Fane's belly cramped with the memory of the sword piercing his flesh. Worse was the pain of it pulling away, out of his reach. He forced himself not to wince. "I didn't lose it. Thorne took it. And I want it back. I'm willing to help you to make that happen."

"The angelic possessed have nothing to offer us besides the abraxas. Without that..." Jonah shrugged.

Fane cracked his knuckles. The other option was to crack said knuckles across Jonah's jutting chin. "I can fight."

"Not like a talya. You'll die."

"Then I'll die."

Jonah studied him. "For a sword?"

Why did people insist angels were so judgmental? They had nothing on the former African missionary man and the teshuva demon glinting violet in his eyes.

Fane let out a sharp breath between his teeth. "When you were maimed, you took on a symballein mate you didn't want to be your right hand, to replace what was no more. And now you would kill for her, die for her."

Jonah spread his left hand wide. "What you say is true. So?"

"I had that myself once, but I lost it—yes, I lost it, out of a weakness I can never defend —and was given the abraxas as recompense. And so I want it back."

After a long moment, the talya jerked his head once, as hard as if Fane had punched him. Was that supposed to be an acknowledgment of some sort? Jonah turned on his boot heel and stalked away, leaving Fane to follow or not.

He followed.

They went upstairs. The old warehouse had been a salvage operation, so the upper level was full of trash and ostensible treasure. A bare space had been cleared in the middle of the clutter except for a dozen mismatched chairs in a circle. A half dozen talyan sat around the child-sized sarcophagus. Why did anyone in Chicago, even demon-ridden warriors, need a sarcophagus of any size? On top of the marble lid was perched a pretty silver tea service with mugs as mismatched as the chairs.

Jonah pointed his hook at one of the empty chairs.

Fane hesitated, waiting for his angel's instincts for trouble to finally rouse. Nothing. With a nod to the talya beside him, he sat.

Nim smirked. "Welcome to a talya coffee klatsch." She handed him a tea cup brimming with a yellow-green liquid. Leaves floated on top. His angel stirred restlessly.

Oh sure, now when they were being friendly his angel warned

him off. Too late.

He tossed back the whole damn cup's worth. And gagged. "Now I know why you need the sarcophagus."

Nim snickered. "Jilly's landlady told us it's an ancient Chinese remedy to stoke your inner fire when it is cold and dark out. Tomorrow night is the longest night of the year, you know."

Fane licked his lips and winced at the sting of cayenne on his tongue. Even as the initial burn waned, the slower spice of ginger glowed within him. He closed his watering eyes for a moment, waiting to spontaneously combust. On the backs of his eyelids, he swore he saw red, red in all shades, like flames dancing, writhing. Which reminded him of Bella... He popped his eyes open to banish the erotic image. "I'm on fire all right."

Around the circle of chairs, the talyan stared dubiously into their cups.

Fane stared back at them. "You mean none of you have tried it yet?"

At the far side of the circle, Ecco—the biggest of the overly large talya, only made bigger by the black tank exposing his broad shoulders—shook his shaved head. "Jilly's landlady is a witch. I'd never drink anything she gave me."

Jonah grinned. "I told you the warden would."

And Jonah had been his vote of confidence? Great. Fane slammed his mug on the tray upside down. "Ex-warden. Which is why I'm here."

Ecco scoffed. "Why would we want you on our side? You're a loser."

After one slow blink to calm himself, Fane said, "Because I have nothing else to lose."

All around the circle, talya heads nodded. Of course, they understood.

The circle came back to Ecco, who lifted one shoulder

infinitesimally. "Can't ever have enough cannon fodder."

That had gone easier than he expected. Fane smiled. "So when are we going after Thorne?"

* * *

He left the warehouse feeling... Well, feeling a little charred. But that was to be expected in the presence of demons, even repentant ones. The second cup of hell tea had added to the sensation. But he thought they would make a place for him, more or less willingly, when they confronted Thorne again.

From the industrial district to Lake Shore Drive which would take him northward and home was a quick jaunt, but he found himself on a more circuitous route through a thin scattering of sleet.

The Mortal Coil was blacker than the @1 warehouse, not a hint of light showing from any of the windows. Even the ouroboros in the circle of stained glass above the door was dim, only its yellow eye still glinting in the darkness. Perhaps he should drive on...

The Porsche stuttered to a halt as if of its own volition.

Fane found himself at the front door. From the angle where he stood, sheltered in the doorway, he caught another glimmer between the black-out curtains drawn over the windows. He ignored the white sign with its rude rejection and knocked.

Nothing. The glimmer cut out and then returned, as if someone had moved between the light source and where he stood. But the door remained stubbornly closed.

The glimmer returned and cut out again. Was Bella trying to come to the door? Was something preventing her? His heartbeat accelerated, and he tried the door knob. Locked. But he'd been in too many fights to let the surge of adrenaline go unused.

He'd also been in enough fights to know the frontal approach wasn't always the best, especially for an angelic possessed going up against demon-ridden whose supernatural sidekicks included perks such as increased speed and strength, not to mention immortality. So he jogged around to the alley.

A beat-up hatchback was parked near the back door, trunk open but empty. He closed it to keep the weather and any other transients out, then ran a hand over the hood: still warm despite the plummeting temperatures.

Sure enough, the back door of the club was unlocked, as if the unloading implied by the open truck had only just completed. Fane pushed through.

The back door was at the end of the bathroom hallway, black except for the red exit sign over his head. His toed thumped something hollow and plastic in the path, which he nudged aside. He strode down the dark hall toward the main room of the club, guided by the intermittent blinking he'd seen from the front step.

He crossed into the cavernous space.

And stopped.

Arrayed around the room at all the entrance points, like the lookouts of a besieged army, were small, nearly identical statues. Most were swathed only from the waist down, and some were molded with their bare, pudgy arms outstretched as if to hold back an enemy, like aggressive half-naked lawn gnomes.

Taken out of context, it was a full heartbeat before Fane recognized them.

It was a platoon of infant Jesuses.

He shook his head, as if he could clear the baffling imagery, but the weird collection remained. Mostly life sized, the effigies had clearly come from a variety of displays. Some had the hard shine of ceramic, though the majority were plastic, and one was transparent, like glass. Fane winced; he'd probably kicked another baby Jesus out of the back door.

From the shadows near the front, a figure emerged. For a second, Fane's heart skipped, and he had the fleeting thought one of the statues had come to life.

But no. Instead of the short, pale, pudgy shape of another modeled infant, Bella—slender and head-to-slippered-toe red—emerged into the blinking light of one of the figurines.

Fane put his hands on his hips. "What the hell?"

Bella unspooled a power cord. "I know, seriously. Why does a baby Jesus need to blink? It even has a frequency dial." She demonstrated on the controller in her hand, cranking up the speed to disco rates.

The statue beside the front door blinked a frantic SOS Fane couldn't decode.

The feeling of cluelessness made him want to lash out, but the cavernous room held only the babies and Bella. "Never mind the blinking." He bit out each word. "Who buys a couple dozen nativity scene Jesuses?"

"Only a crazy person, obviously." She dropped the cord but didn't leave the tangle of reaching white arms. "So you think I'm crazy?"

At first he thought the twist of her lips was self-deprecating. But when he parsed her tone, he decided she only meant she hadn't bought them at all. What sort of evil person would *steal* baby Jesuses right out of their mangers?

He took a hard step toward her, letting his boot heels ring on the floor so she would hear he was pissed. "Let me guess. This some sort of theme party you're planning, something so sacrilegious you had to close the club so you could invite only the worst sort of pathetic deviants."

"No." She crossed her arms, plumping up her breasts into the deep scoop of her long-sleeved shirt. The red and orange stripes bowed and the front buttons bulged under the pressure of her agitated breathing. He might have thought she was mocking his own similar stance except he knew she couldn't see him. "There's no party. No one else is invited." She tilted her head, making him pointedly aware he was included among that no one.

Since a sick house party was the only reasonable explanation, he was left with nothing. To think, he'd wanted to stop by and see her, to see how she was doing after...after their encounter, and to thank her for passing his message to the talyan through Nanette and sharing the tip on Sera's demon-sensitive father. He rather suspected the suggestion had mellowed the talyan toward him, for no good reason but he appreciated the opportunity and wondered how she'd known that little trick.

But now here he was, facing a more twisted mystery. If only he'd been content with the one-night stand.

"Walk away." Her low voice seemed to thrum in his chest, almost an echo of his thoughts. "Just leave."

He wanted to, he really did. But though he'd lost his abraxas and the sphericanum had revoked his warden rank, he still shared himself with a divine presence. He couldn't let this outrage pass.

He took another step toward her. "You know I won't go. This is a mockery, not just of the symbols but the spirit of a holy season."

"I wasn't mocking. I needed them."

"No one needs a couple dozen Jesuses."

She sniffed. "More than a couple dozen branches of Christianity would say *you* are being sacrilegious."

Through clenched teeth, he emphasized, "You can't steal Jesus."

"Actually, I stole a bunch of them."

"And you'll be taking them back. Get your friend in here and start loading them up."

She wrinkled her nose, making her glasses lift and shine the blinking baby's light at him. "What friend?" She looked as confused as he felt.

"Your wheel man, whoever helped you carry off the statues." Fane steeled himself against a ridiculous surge of jealousy. She had asked someone else for help when he'd been here only a few nights ago. Of course, he wouldn't have helped her steal from nativity scenes, but she hadn't even bothered to hint she had more sins in mind than what they'd shared.

Bella shook her head. "There's nobody else here. No friend."

The bitterness in her tone rang true to the unpleasant spite he struggled to subdue. Which meant… "You drove yourself? Then you're not…"

She turned away. "I don't know where you all got the idea I was blind."

He closed the distance between them in three strides and yanked her back around, the slender muscles of her arm tight under his fingers. She kept her face averted, but the blinking light caught the clouded white cataracts in her eyes. "We thought it because that's the impression you gave us. You're a thief *and* a liar?"

She lifted her chin finally. "I don't know where you got the impression I was anything but."

"You've been helping the talyan."

"Will you leave me alone about this? I don't see things the way you do—"

Frustration and disappointment jolted through his muscles, making his restraining grasp spring open. His lip curled. "Clearly not, if you think what you've done here is in any way justifiable."

Rather than escape, she swung toward him. "Oh, so *tonight* you want to get on Santa's nice list?"

The reference, even oblique, to their previous encounter made his face flush—his whole body, really—and knowing she could see it only mixed his embarrassment with anger.

"We're taking them back, all of them, to wherever you stole them," he snarled.

She straightened, her jaw set, even though her red fuzzy slippers rather undermined the intensity of her resistance. "I won't."

"I'll make you."

"You can't."

"Watch me." He marched around her and headed toward the blinking baby Jesus.

"No!" Bella grabbed his arm, but her slippers had no traction on the dance floor and he hauled her onward. "You can't!" This time, her tone was less refusal and more desperation. "I need them. It's almost the solstice."

She'd said that before. "If you want Christmas decorations, you can buy your own. I'll loan you the money. You can repay me…" Well, that came out of him a little more suggestively than he'd intended.

But she didn't taunt him, just hauled more urgently at his arm. "It won't be the same. These have meaning, they've been given meaning."

"Yes, meaning for other people. And you can't steal sentiment. You have to make your own connection to the heart and soul of the season."

"You don't understand. I can't."

The way she'd sounded when she'd said she had no friend made him hesitate. He glanced down at her as she stared up. Her lips were slightly parted with her distress, her fingers a warm insistence on his arm, and her eyes glinted. Maybe just a reflection of the burglarized blinking baby, but maybe tears.

He stopped. "I can help you find the way."

"You?" She laughed, shrill, like a needle skipping on a record, and let him go. "You and your angel? Without your lighted sword?"

He stiffened at the disbelief in her tone and the tinge of loss he felt as the sensation of her touch faded. "With or without the abraxas, I'll make sure you do the right thing."

"You can't." She spun around him to block his way toward the statues and held out one hand, her slender fingers spread like a pale star against the darkness behind her.

Her insistence held a note of panic that gave him pause, but he had already drifted once from the path with her. Without his abraxas, he was vulnerable—in more ways than one. "The right thing is what I do." And it was all he had.

Bella shook her head violently, threatening to bring down the red tower of her hair. "You can't take them. They are the only wall holding back the demons coming for me!"

Despite his heavy wool coat and the flush of his anger, a chill rippled across Fane's skin, seeming to enter where her touch had left. "If demons are coming, we'll stop them. You have to deny them, not give them a place in your soul—"

"Soul?" Her whisper fell with hollow despair. "I don't have one."

The chill sank deeper, through his skin, past his bones, into the indiscernible place where the angel dwelled. "What do you mean?"

"I don't have a soul." On the last word, her voice dropped lower, breaking into eerie double octaves: demonic harmonics. "I am one of them."

CHAPTER 5

"I am one of them." The confession—demonically spoken—tore at Bella's throat.

She grimaced at the need for truth. It tasted like blood. She was being a bit melodramatic; the old-copper-penny tang was merely the demon damage done to her human tissue. But if she didn't tell him, he would take the Jesuses and she would have nothing to hold back the longest night.

In ominous silence, Fane reached out to her. Maybe he meant to grab only her chin, but with his big hand, his fingers overlapped to her neck, his thumb pressed hard to the point of her jaw. The charge of conflicting energies made her wince at the new pain, but she didn't pull away. With his angel roused, he could very well kill her.

By tradition, that's what angels did to demons.

He turned her chin from one side to the other. His gold-sparked gaze sparked in her demon-compromised vision; demons might not see every aspect of the mortal realm clearly, but they were well adapted to recognize—and fear—angels. "You are not a talya," he said at last. "I would know."

As if having been buried balls-deep in her cunt gave him some special insight?

She decided not to say that aloud. "I am not teshuva. There are other kinds of demons."

The horde-tenebrae came in many flavors—malice, feralis, salambe, djinni—each darker than the last. But he knew that. His grip tightened until she felt her carotid pulse banging against his fingers. "Then what are you?"

She opened her mouth and the word came out in a curl of frozen air. To the divine presence possessing him, she knew it was a nasty, craven sound, and her heart curdled to say it. To the human ear, the meaning was simple: "Imp."

"Imp," he repeated. Somehow, he managed to make it sound even worse. His thin, masculine lips—which had been so hot and possessive all over her skin—twisted in disgust.

She coughed a little, from the strangling power of his grip and the wounds in her throat. A spot of blood stained the white cuff of his shirt poking out beyond his coat sleeve.

He recoiled, letting her loose.

She wiped her mouth but didn't try to run. Where would she go? The longest night was almost here, and this was the only place she could barricade herself.

"Why did the talyan not see you for a demon?" he demanded.

She touched the corner of her glasses and blinked over the cataracts occluding her corneas. "My eyes. Windows to the soul, you know. Well, my windows are dirty. No one can see in."

"But you are human. I felt you..." To her demon senses, the blood flowing through his cheeks was unmistakable and tantalizing.

"The body is human. I am...not. Not exactly, not anymore."

"Explain."

"I..." She sighed. "Can we go up to my apartment where it's more comfortable?"

His bark of laughter echoed through the shadows. "By all means, let's get comfortable now."

Dread—and his no-doubt furious glower—tightened the muscles between her shoulder blades as she led the way to the back staircase. Two identical baby Jesuses flanked the doorway, and she flinched at Fane's explosive curse. There were two more—twins again, though in a different style—at the top of the stairs. She couldn't stop herself from touching the hard ringlets of their plastic hair; she needed their protection a little earlier than she had expected. But—except for the fact their arms were already up, reaching in the classic baby Jesus pose—they probably wouldn't lift a hand to protect her from an avenging angel.

She led Fane into her apartment, the last place she'd wanted him. There was a reason she'd fucked him on the bar counter. The addition of another dozen Jesuses only made the profusion of religious and spiritual paraphernalia more insane looking.

Russian icons plastered the walls between Tibetan prayer flags interspersed with fragments of ancient Torahs. Small figurines of Christian saints shared Wiccan altar space with Hindu gods and Kachina dolls. Islamic prayer rugs covered every inch of the floor and softened her steps. The bed, half hidden by a freestanding Buddhist triptych, was plumped with grandma-style throw pillows embroidered with quasi-religious affirmations. The open loft extended half the space of the bar below, though it looked smaller crammed with all the holy crap.

In the middle of the room, he turned a slow circle, hands on his hips.

She didn't want to see his expression, not even the little details her altered vision granted her. "Do you want a drink?"

"No. Not after the last one you poured me."

"Well, I need one." She headed for the galley kitchen with its eating bar overlooking the living space. At the sink, she rinsed out her mouth and spat out pink froth. Not for the first time she envied the talyan their strong teshuva demons that healed as often as they hurt. An imp had nowhere near such power. Not that she deluded herself into thinking an angel would overlook her merely for her insignificance.

She mixed herself a cocktail from the mini bar she kept stocked from the bar's supplies. She tossed back the first drink, cringing at the alcohol sting in her throat. Then she mixed another.

"You drink a lot," Fane said, a grudging note in his voice, as if he couldn't stop his angelic nature from commenting even on her little sins.

"I have good reasons. Or bad reasons, I suppose." She hitched herself up onto the kitchen counter and crossed her legs.

He shifted his jaw, no doubt remembering the last time she'd been up on a counter. He kept his attention focused across the room, like maybe it'd be harder to slay her if he had to think about their evening together. Well, fuck him.

Oh, wait. She had.

She took another drink.

Finally, he turned back to her. "An imp is a lesser incorporeal tenebrae. It doesn't have the possessive power of a teshuva or djinni. How did it take up residence in your body?"

Thanks to the sphericanum, he'd know enough about demons that she wouldn't have to explain every stupid detail. How convenient. "This is not *my* body," she said. "I *am* only the imp. There's no soul here. Elvis has left the building."

"How?"

She clutched the drink until the faceted edges of the glass grated against bone. "I killed her."

A long, slow breath whistled from him, like the sound a descending fiery sword might make as it aimed for her neck. She supposed she should be glad Thorne had taken Fane's abraxas. She could only hope to appeal to the compassionate angel inside him.

Just the thought almost made her laugh. Or cry. Crying had been the first thing she'd done in this body.

She swallowed more of the drink. "No, I guess that's not quite true. The imp didn't kill her. She intended to kill herself, and the imp was one of the horde drawn to her anguish."

"Why didn't you…" Fane fell silent.

"Why didn't I stop her? I had no 'I' then. Just the imp, and it had no thoughts as you would understand them. The tenebrae are only ravening hunger and fury and obliteration. Of course they—we—were drawn to Mirabel and all the pain and grief gouging her. We yearned for a place to be, a place where we could hide from the tenebraeternum, and she had such a vast emptiness inside her."

Fane was quiet a moment, then he said, "I want that drink now."

Bella reached behind her for the open bottles and poured. He stood as far away from her as he could and still reach the glass. She tried not to let his distance hurt. She was a monster, after all.

"It happened up here," she said. "This was a storage room at the time, and Mirabel was a waitress downstairs. It was on the solstice—the bar stayed open all through Christmas back then—and she had bruises from one guy who kept pinching her ass, but he tipped really good. That's one of my first memories…" She stared down at her drained glass.

"What happened?" Fane's soft question loosened her tongue more than the alcohol.

"I…Mirabel had come up here to restock the booze and to take a pain pill. She kept her drugs hidden behind a loose board over there." Bella jerked her chin toward an old reliquary tucked into a wall nook. "She wanted to sit down for a minute, to rest her feet, but her butt cheeks were sore. So she stood, looking out over there—" She gestured toward the narrow, mullioned window. "It was snowing a little, maybe enough for a white Christmas, maybe not. Out of nowhere, she decided to take the whole bottle of pills." Bella paused. "No, not out of nowhere. The tenebrae—we—had been focused on her for awhile." She forced herself to look at Fane. "And you know what the tenebrae presence does."

He nodded and took a long drink.

"She hadn't gone home for Christmas in years. She'd just broken up with the last in a long line of shitty boyfriends who'd stiffed her on the rent. She had nowhere to be and no one waiting for her. So she swallowed all the pills, chased them down with half a bottle of vodka. And then she used her box cutter." Bella dragged up her sleeves and tilted both forearms toward him.

Slowly, he approached. His thigh bumped her knee, and she inhaled the sweet scent of the Drambuie she'd poured him. He ran one finger down the raised scar on her left arm. "No hesitation marks. This wasn't a cry for help. She was done."

Bella shivered, at his touch or his words or the memories, she wasn't sure. "If she'd ever cried out, only the demons noticed. And we drank her misery like it was last call."

She hurled her glass. It hit the wall beside the reliquary and shattered.

"Fuck," she said, apropos of nothing.

Fane did not even twitch when the glass sailed by his ear. "But you're here. Which means she didn't die."

"She did. The imp watched while her eyes misted, as if the escaping soul was clawing free of the body, like a diamond scarring glass. The imp—I—wanted more. I wanted all of her agony. I wanted to dance in the light fading from her eyes. I got too close. As her soul left, I felt the emptiness sucking at me. The imp tried to flee, but it was too late. It sucked me right in. And I was born into her. I was born, dying."

She shuddered. "The imp got misery in spades that night. I puked up the booze and pills. I wrapped my arms in bar rags and staggered downstairs. You can imagine the mayhem. Joy to the fucking world."

"And so Mirabel became Bella."

"I took everything of hers: her body, her memories, her speech patterns, her fashion sense, her wheat allergy. I even took her last loser boyfriend so I could give him a taste of the demon tongue, though he barely heard his long litany of sins over his screaming. After all I took, I thought I should at least leave her name."

"Nice of you."

She flinched. "I am a monster, a monster in a dead girl's clothing. But the one thing Mirabel didn't give me, the one thing the imp brought with it, is this: I am not going back to hell."

Fane inclined his head. "Not unless I send you there."

CHAPTER 6

Fane refused to let her sudden blanching sway him. Poor Mirabel had needed help and sympathy. This creature before him deserved none of that.

Slowly, Bella slid off the counter. Since he did not move back, she stood toe to toe with him. In her slippers, the top of her red beehive barely reached his nose, and she had to tilt her head to look up at him. "You won't have to do a damned thing to me. The tenebrae are coming, like they do every year on the darkest night. If you take my defenses, I am worse than dead."

It had always been a point of curiosity to the sphericanum that the tenebrae—for all the demons decided lack of repenting—fled from their dismal realm into the human world at any opportunity. Even demons didn't want to live in hell. But he supposed they wouldn't want one of their own living the good life either.

He stared down at her with grim foreboding, his whole body tight with shock, as if waiting for another blow.

She was tenebrae. How could he have been so blind? The irony of the thought did not escape him, but even knowing what he did now, his angel couldn't find the demon in her eyes. He saw only the blue-white shine of the cataracts. "How can the tenebraeternum be worse than death?"

"Is an angel-man even allowed to ask?" The defiant set of her shoulders wavered. "For a while, I hoped Mirabel's history would erase the imp's recollections of its own realm, but in some ways, the two were so similar: the emptiness, the desolation, the conviction it would always be that way. Mirabel used the booze and drugs and cutter to escape her own version of hell. The imp fled the tenebraeternum into the space she left behind." She wrapped her arms around herself. "Now I have both their memories. And it's worse this time of year."

He focused on the religious mayhem behind her, anything to avoid looking at her as he struggled to come to grips with this unwelcome truth. He tightened one hand into a fist until he remembered the feel of the fine bones of her neck under his fingers, then his hand sprang open of its own accord. "All the spiritual artifacts. You use them to repel the tenebrae."

"This body protects me from the effects of the artifacts, but my cousins still hate the flavors of hope, joy and love."

That was the sanctuary the artifacts offered her? A wall of joy and hope? He'd never thought of his abraxas in such a way. A warden's holy relic was always a weapon, an object of carnage and terror. Love couldn't hold a killing edge.

He stalked away from her and prowled the room, stopping at the window where another baby Jesus looked out into the night, much as Mirabel must have done.

He stared down at it. "It's just plastic."

From behind him, Bella said, "I've heard it's the thought that counts."

"People say so only because they got you a shitty present."

"You know better. People imbue objects with their beliefs. Which is why I can't use Santas to guard the way. I don't want the tenebrae coming for me as their gift."

He turned his glare on her. "But Jesus died for our sins, so you don't have to?"

She lifted her chin. "That is one aspect of their faith, yes. What's so wrong about that?"

"Let's ask Mirabel." He grabbed the statue and headed for the next one.

"You can't take them!" Bella rushed around the edge of the counter toward him.

He lifted one hand—the one without the baby Jesus tucked under it—and forced his angel to rise in a glow of gold around his knuckles. "You took them. I'm taking them back."

She skidded to a halt, her mouth twisted. "You want me to die, don't you?"

"No. But I won't let you lie and steal either. If you want to atone for the imp, you start now."

"The longest night of the year is coming, the night she died. The tenebrae *will* come."

"Let them come. We will stand against them."

She lowered her chin, doubt obvious in the tight pull of her mouth, but she didn't back away from him. "One imp in the body of a dead girl and one angel in exile?"

He did not bother explaining how he would soon retrieve his abraxas. Yes, he was going to have to make some compromises, but only for the greater good. "We aren't alone. The talyan—"

She laughed, and he had to admit, claiming common cause with the league was rather absurd. "The only ones who hate the tenebrae more than the sphericanum are the teshuva," she reminded him. "They followed us to their doom and now they repent with our slaughter."

"You aren't tenebrae," he shot back. "Not anymore."

"At least they still want me. The talyan certainly won't." She sidled closer to him. "But maybe you want me again. Is that the concession you're looking for?"

He tightened his jaw at her sideways smile. "I'm not looking for anything."

"You didn't just happen to drive through this neighborhood." She reached out and popped open the top button of his shirt.

"And you are not wearing anything underneath this time. I wonder why when it's so cold outside."

Rampant heat rushed through him: mortification—how had she known when he hadn't realized the inference, not until this very moment?—and lust. Her finger stroked the notch of his throat, and he swallowed.

So close, the perfume of her made his head spin, a potent tease of vodka, womanly flesh and—so his angel warned him—a hidden peril like a hint of smoke. She hooked her finger through his second button and leaned in to press her lips over the pounding of his pulse.

His lips parted, against his will anticipating her caress, but he would not lower his head.

She undid the second button and kissed the bare skin above his heart. "How about one orgasm for each Jesus, hmm? Seems fair."

"Actually, that seems impious." He reared back, grabbing her wrist when she sneakily tried to snatch at the statue under his arm.

"*Imp*ious? Oh, you're a laugh riot." She lunged at him. "Damn it, Cyril. Give it to me!"

"No." He stiff-armed her. "You told me people give meaning to their artifacts. That body you wield with such insolence is your reliquary now. So make it mean something."

She stood staring at him, her hands fisted, her muscles drawn so tight the scars on her exposed wrists writhed. Finally, she said, "I can't."

He turned his back on her and began collecting the Jesuses.

Her demonic double-tongued wail of despair followed him downstairs and dogged him out to the Porsche where he tried to stack the infants neatly, but after several trips he still ended up with something like a holy midget clown car. What the hell was he going to do with them all?

He hadn't prayed since his abraxas was taken, but he reminded himself not to speed since getting stopped by a cop would result in some awkward explaining.

He belted himself in and stared up through the sunroof to the upper window of the bar. Dark and empty. He dragged his hand over his mouth to erase the phantom sensation of the kiss she hadn't given him.

He revved up the engine—the only thing getting any action tonight—and slammed the Porsche into gear.

And just as quickly slammed on the breaks.

Lit by the bright headlights, Bella all in red shone like a wayward flame.

Fane closed his eyes for a moment and tried to find the divine stillness within. He was an angelic possessed minus his abraxas, cut off from the guiding hands of the sphericanum; could he trust himself to know a right choice even if it was standing right in front of him?

He cracked one eye. *She* was still standing right in front of him.

The wild blaze of her against the white streaks of sleet only quickened the furious thud of his heart. He wanted to help her. And he wanted her. The conflicting impulses warred in him. Would the right impulse win? As likely as a snowball's chance in Chicago in August.

* * *

Without a word, they followed the maps she'd printed and marked up with cryptic notes. At each stop, they got out, she selected an infant, and they returned the missing messiah to his adoring and apparently oblivious worshippers. At first, Fane didn't believe she could match them all, but each scene was a little different from the others and each baby perfectly fit. Plastic or wood, ceramic or inflated, each found their home.

"Last one," he said after hours had passed.

She bent over the final page of her printouts and scrawled an X before handing it to him; obviously it had been an unscheduled stop. He took the map, noted the address, and rolled his eyes. "You stole from the nursing home?"

She stared out the side window without answering.

He tried to hold onto his outrage, but it was late. And at least she was here: sullen and silent, but here. "You can't fight off evil by being bad." He imagined Mirabel's deadbeat ex-boyfriend, facing the imp's guilty fury; that was less a measure of justice than a shot of revenge. And Bella's occasional assistance to the league was self-serving at best. He refused to wonder how his own involvement with the talyan might appear to the impartial observer. "We have to hold the line. It's all we can do."

"The only thing we can do." Her low voice sounded raw, hurt. "I notice you don't say it's a good thing."

He tightened his grip on the steering wheel, wondering if he should be pleased she'd said *we*. "Only thing, good thing, whatever."

"Whatever."

He wondered if the doomed Mirabel had spoken that same word in that same hollow tone. Guilt nipped at him. As an angelic possessed, he was supposed to show the way to salvation. Before, he'd mostly hacked a path, machete-style. But he didn't have his sword now.

"You have a unique opportunity here," he told her. "The teshuva and the djinn don't really communicate with their hosts. No one knows why the demons lends all their powers but none of their knowledge. You may be the only ex-tenebrae in existence with a voice."

"I have nothing anyone would want to hear."

"Maybe that used to be true, but the Chicago talyan are

different from any league that has come before. They are willing to take the fight beyond what this world has known, and they could use all the help they can get."

She faced him, her jaw off-kilter with rebelliousness. "Even from an imp?"

"Their demons are repentant, remember? Which means they were wrong first."

"I've tried to give them hints where I could, tell them what I've seen of the tenebrae." She tugged at one of the loose curls of red hair hanging beside her cheek and coiled it around her finger. He realized the boldness was only a frail mask over her anxiety, as distracting and delicate as her antique glasses. "Obviously I can't tell them I've seen too much since their task is to eradicate monsters like me."

"You are not a monster." The words came out more harshly than he intended.

She flinched, but the hard set of her chin didn't waver. "The imp I was swallowed more darkness than every winter night you can remember times a thousand. You might be angel-ridden, but you have no inkling how bad evil can be."

Silence returned.

The nursing home was dark, closed up tight, when they drifted to a stop at the sidewalk. The spitting snow had gone, but the cold seemed more bitter for it. Fane hunched into his coat and strode around the front of the car to let Bella out. She already had the last statue.

For an instant, the sight of her cradling the infant with its upraised arms—Madonna and sinner in one—froze him in his tracks with a memory colder and more bitter than even the Chicago winter wind.

Bella glanced up when he did not move out of the way. She frowned. "Cyril?"

The dead shine of her eyes and his name on her lips, wary and miserable, went through him like a sword of ice. He took a step back, slamming his spine into the edge of the door.

"What's wrong?"

"Nothing." His voice sounded hoarse, shaken. He swallowed hard. "It's three in the morning and I'm un-stealing religious statuary with a demon. A demon I fucked. What could be wrong?"

She tucked her head down and slipped out of the car, avoiding him. The power cord dangled behind her like a severed umbilical.

He turned away, bracing himself on the frame of the car. The breath caught in his throat, freezing and jagged as the ice floes shoved up on the lakeshore by the relentless wind. He closed his eyes.

Through his tight-clenched eyes, a pale glow intruded. Reluctantly, he glanced over his shoulder.

In the middle of the plastic nativity set, Bella had plugged in the baby Jesus, and the off-white light blinked. She knelt to adjust the controller before tucking the infant in, and the light steadied. Fane averted his gaze from her bowed red head, the only color in the ghostly tableau.

"Fane." Her soft call stiffened his shoulders.

If she thought he was going to let her keep the last one... "Let's go."

"Something's wrong."

"I told you already—"

"I don't care what's wrong with *you* now. Get your head out of your ass and let your angel eyes out. Something is wrong here."

Hands fisted against the bottoms of his coat pockets, he stalked across the lawn. "If they see us out here—"

"Never mind what they'll see." She rocked back on her heels, revealing the manger where she'd been about to put the statuette. "What do *you* see?"

He blinked back the sting in his eyes from the rising wind, but the oily sheen of the glass orb where the baby should have been nestled writhed sickeningly in his vision. "What the hell?"

She nodded. "There's a soul bomb in the manger."

Chapter 7

Fane immediately called the league despite Bella's half-hearted protest. "If the bomb releases soul shards, it'll bring tenebrae from all directions, you know that," he told her. "The teshuva can contain the damage."

She wrapped her arms around herself though nothing seemed to stop the chills wracking her. "I know. Just...please don't tell them..." She tucked her chin into her coat. "I don't want the damage they contain to be *me*."

Fane lifted his chin and studied her down the length of his clearly-never-been-punched-hard-enough nose. "You have to tell them eventually."

Why, when they hadn't figured it out yet? But she didn't say that. "I know," she repeated. "But I want to do it my own way." When his expression didn't change, she added, "I want to do it right."

That seemed to mollify him, at least for the moment. Anyway, he was too busy making calls on his cell phone. While he did, she walked the perimeter of the building, and when she returned, he was standing with his hands on his hips, staring impatiently at her.

"Four more," she told him. "Quite a bit bigger than this, and they are all wired. Looks like a mess of trigger, timer and accelerometer." She angled her face away. "Guess it's a good thing we stopped by."

He mumbled something she wasn't sure she wanted to decipher.

She was spared any need to reply when the porch light blinked on.

"I called Nanette too," Fane said. "She'll need to know everything."

Bella huffed out an exasperated breath to obscure her flicker of dismay. She didn't get much chance to cultivate attachments with other people, and the angel-woman had been kind enough. While Nanette had seemingly forgiven the talyan for their role in her husband's murder, would she be so merciful toward a creature of the tenebraeternum? "Don't tell her about me either. She'll have enough to worry about."

He nodded once, curtly, and strode toward the other angelic possessed. Bella didn't want to be surrounded by their flickering golden stares, but neither did she particularly want to wait at the street for the talyan who were no doubt gunning their crappy cars en route even as she dithered.

She followed Fane.

Nanette pulled the door half shut behind her and wrung her hands. "How did this happen?"

"We don't know." Fane glanced at Bella. They might not know how, but they did know when. The soul bombs hadn't been in place when she took the baby Jesus. Not that a timeline helped them particularly.

Nanette clutched her housecoat around her. "Do we need to evacuate? We're understaffed, but I can call in nurses and families."

Bella cleared her throat. "If it was a real bomb, maybe. But if the tenebrae are targeting the home, moving everyone will just add to the chaos. Adding to the chaos is never a good idea when dealing with the horde. Better to hunker down." She slanted an accusing stare at Fane.

He ignored her. "We need to check the interior too. I want to find every orb."

Nanette waved them inside. "How can this be happening again? Corvus was defeated."

"But evil wasn't," Bella said. As if to underscore her point, a trio of beat-up @1 sedans turned the corner, targeting the nursing home like mangy sharks. "Why don't you walk me around?"

The angel-woman nodded distractedly, and Bella didn't look back as the talyan poured out to confront Fane.

Inside, the home was almost ridiculously warm and smelled of cinnamon. Despite the fear and anger that had torqued through her since Fane's return to the Mortal Coil, Bella felt her tension ease. She slipped out of her parka and left it on the bench by the front door.

"I can't believe you two found these things," Nanette said as they crossed into the spacious living area.

"Believe it," Bella murmured. "Does Sera's father go outside?"

"Not so often when the weather is bad. Why?"

The old preacher had noticed something amiss. "What does he do when he's inside?"

"Well, he watches TV here with the others and takes meals in the dining room, of course. And he likes to watch the fish in the aquarium."

Bella peered into the unlit gas fireplace. Nothing. "Fish, hmm? Show me."

Nanette led her around the far side of the living area toward the dining room. "Here, where everyone can enjoy them."

"Yeah, everyone." Bella circled the large freshwater tank. "See anything new?"

"Honestly, I'm not sure I'd—Oh. Oh no."

The glass orb in the tank wasn't as large as any of the others, but it had the same oily gleam, though the fish seemed unbothered. They cruised past the slowly roiling surface, their jewel tones distorted and weird.

Bella sighed.

"They were in here," Nanette whispered. "The demons were in here."

Bella pursed her lips. "The demons are everywhere." She lifted the lid on the tank.

Nanette shifted uneasily. "Maybe we should leave it…"

"I think we were supposed to find it. Otherwise, why put it in such a public spot?" She wondered whether the bomber had been rushed, bored, out of souls, or what, that they'd only found a half dozen of the weapons. Certainly she should be able to ascertain a motive. After all, she was a monster too. She wriggled her fingers to expel the shakes. "Besides, if it goes off, the talyan are already here."

The fish fled as she slid her hands through the cool water. She touched the orb's surface carefully but found none of the wires of the versions outside. It did, however, feel as slimy as it looked, though nothing obvious slicked off on her fingers. She lifted the dripping ball from the tank, half tensed for a kaboom. But the oily luster continued its slow-motion boil across the surface, uninterrupted.

Nanette stared at the bomb, nibbling her bottom lip. "Maybe we should break it. Shouldn't the souls be freed? It's wrong to keep them imprisoned."

"How very angelic of you," Bella said. "But let's stay down-to-earth for a little while longer, okay?"

She headed for the home's activity room where Fane and the talyan had convened.

Nanette pulled the double doors shut behind them and faced the talyan. "Bella found one bomb inside. In the fish tank."

Talya eyebrows shot up as Bella displayed the fist-sized orb, but the littlest talya—Alyce, who had come to the league as a rogue—

nodded. "Thorne."

Fane stiffened. "How can we be sure?"

Alyce shrugged and leaned against Sidney, her Bookkeeper mate, who wrapped his arm around her waist. "Thorne was a bomb maker in his solely human days life. And he likes fish."

"Then why—?" Fane rubbed the bridge of his nose. "Never mind. So how do we spring this trap on him?"

Sid frowned. "I consider myself a fairly clever fellow, but I don't think I follow."

"Obviously Thorne intends this to be trouble for the league. He obviously chose this place because of your connection to it. So how can we reverse this, lure him in, use the souls against him, so I can...so we can end him, once and for all?"

Talya eyebrows rose even higher, and Bella too wondered at the words Fane left out.

"Warden," Nanette said, with just a hint of shock in her voice. "We can't put the residents at risk."

"Ex-warden," Fane snapped. But he seemed to sense the disapproval coming from the talyan as well. "There wouldn't be much additional risk, considering this season is already spiritually difficult time for some people—"

"Fucker!" Bella punched him.

Or meant to. She wished she'd swung first, then yelled at him, because he ducked, catching her fist on the heavy padding of his coat.

He caught her second swing too and spun her into the steely cage of his arms. "What the hell?"

She bobbled the orb, making the talyan gasp. "Hell is exactly what you'd bring down on them, you cruel, egotistical, *evil* asshole. And you think I'm the—" She choked on her own fury and almost stupid slip.

Fane tightened his grip when she thrashed against his hold.

"Calm down, Bella. You'll break the orb. Or wake up the old people."

"And you'd rather have them innocent and defenseless in their beds!"

"No one is innocent." His low growl thrummed through her body, like a reminder exactly how innocent she wasn't. "And they won't be defenseless either, now that we're here."

He spun her away from him, and she staggered a few steps. Despite his brusque dismissal, he kept a grip on her wrist and didn't let go.

Liam Niall—the big, steady leader of the league, who'd been the first of the talyan to see she was something more than a bartender, though he'd never pushed her to reveal more and she had never offered—watched them under hooded eyes, arms crossed over his wide blacksmith chest. "This is all very odd."

She didn't want him to think how odd, so she hurried to distract them. "It's odder than you might have first seen." Fane's grasp tightened, driving tendon to bone, and she hissed. "Those aren't soul shards in the orbs. I think the bombs are packed with tenebrae."

The stifled uproar was bad enough that Nanette shushed them this time. "Unless you want to make breakfast for a dozen seniors. And I warn you, they all want their eggs cooked differently."

Ecco flexed his biceps, making the razor-embedded gauntlets on his forearms bristle. "I only do scrambled."

The exchange quieted the gathering, then Liam pinned Bella with a thoughtful stare. "So tell me your theory." Despite his contemplative tone, his eyes churned with violet highlights, his teshuva on the prowl.

She swallowed back the chalky taste of her nervousness. She had dealt with talyan before. Usually by getting them drunk, but still. "The energy is wrong. You can feel it."

"I can't," Fane said, grievance sharpening his tone.

She refused to look at him. "Nanette, repeat what you said when I pulled the orb out of the tank."

The angel-woman frowned. "I don't...I wondered if we should let the souls go."

"Not yet," Fane grumbled under his breath. "Not until we get Thorne."

Bella shook him off and took a step closer to Nanette. "Why did you wonder that?"

"Because even if they are just shards, even if these are remnants from the solvo drug that tore people's souls apart, it's wrong to lock them away." She wiped her eyes, but conviction rang in her voice. "They need to pass on, to find their way to a better place."

With each heartfelt word, Bella advanced. And as she got closer to the angelic possessed, the ugly clouds on the orb swirled faster and darker, disturbed. The clouds circled away from the side nearest Nanette, as if the inhabitants tried to flee from her presence but couldn't get far in the confines of the orb.

"Whatever's inside doesn't want her sympathy," Liam noted.

Bella rolled a meaningful glare toward Fane. "Which is why you didn't notice anything. They are responding to her compassion and gentleness, her love..."

He tilted his chin up in that arrogant way that seemed to put him out of her reach. "Demons don't know love."

"Yes, they do," she countered. "And they know it has power over them, which is why they are trying to get *away*, not *to* her."

Liam nodded slowly. "The orbs here are nothing like the soul bombs Corvus blew out of glass. Those were almost beautiful, but these... If this is Thorne's work, he has taken the fight to a new level."

Fane crossed his arms. "Soul or demon, it doesn't matter. The end result in either case will be too many tenebrae in one place, with all the pandemonium that entails."

Bella echoed his stance with her hands fisted on her hips. "And you think we should use the pandemonium against Thorne?"

"Corvus proved the tenebrae can be commanded." Then he gave her an assessing look she didn't much like.

The talyan, seemingly oblivious to the undercurrents, were discussing among themselves.

"If only we had a mobile app version of the verge," Sid mused in his oh-so-proper British accent. "If the bombs go off, the verge could swallow the tenebrae en masse as they broke out of the orbs."

Bella couldn't restrain a shudder. She'd heard the talyan talk about the verge, a portal into the tenebraeternum that had formed when Corvus Valerius sought to instigate direct war between heaven and hell. Although Corvus had intended to call forth the tenebrae, the talyan had claimed the portal occupying a dank basement at Navy Pier and managed to stuff more than one demon back down hell's throat. She'd never seen it herself and never wanted to. The thought of being banished back to the tenebraeternum… It was everything she dreaded.

Ecco scratched his gauntlets across the back of his head with the sound of sandpaper. "Mini pocket hells. Like purse dogs, except instead of bacon bits, they eat demons. I can't believe we didn't think of that before."

"No need to be sarcastic," Sid chastised. "See, it's making the demons dance."

Bella stared down at the orb. It did indeed look 'happier,' if the steaks of pus yellow and mucous green churning over its surface were any indication. But was it the talya's sarcasm or her own sickly churning stomach reflected in the glass?

She tossed the orb to Fane. "It's all yours, angel-man."

He swore and caught it gingerly, cushioning its fall with cupped hands. She couldn't help but notice he was more tender with the bomb than he'd been with her.

She refused to wonder if she was being unfair. Instead, she headed for the closed double doors and let herself out.

"Wait." Nanette hurried after her. "Where are you going?"

"I can't help here." She went to the front bench and collected her coat. "The bombs, the verge, it's out of my league." Out of her league, maybe, but very much of her legion, the legions of darkness. She stared out through the leaded glass windows of the front door. The rectangles of framed night looked even blacker to her imp eyes.

God, why did the nights have to be so long?

"The buses won't be running," Nanette said. "Let me call you a cab this time."

Bella nodded numbly.

"No." Fane's sharp denial was like a crack against the thin wall of her restraint. One more nudge and her own demon would come pouring out… "I'll take her home."

Yeah, there was the nudge.

She whirled to face him. "I don't want you." Her tone rang with the truth. And with the lie. Damn the demon's double tongue.

Nanette clasped her hands in front of her. "Mr. Fane, it's been a troubling night. I think maybe you should—"

"Ward." His eyes glimmered with the gold sparks of his roused angel. "Your kind heart is not needed here."

"Ex-warden," she replied, much more mildly but with equal gold admonition. "A kind heart is always needed."

Bella tensed. Was she going to have to jump into the middle of an angel war right here? Could this night get any worse?

After a long moment, Fane smiled tightly. It wasn't a beatific smile of the sort favored by saints. It was more the sort an avenging angel gave as he listened to the blood of his enemies snap-crackle-pop on his flaming sword. "I think we have both been around the talyan too long. We have forgotten what we are."

But Nanette did not soften. "I have not forgotten." She touched Bella's arm. "Shall I call that cab?"

Though she desperately wanted to take the angel-woman's offer, Bella felt the weight of Fane's glower like that missing sword dangling above her head. And she didn't particularly want to leave him with the talyan. Who knew what he might tell them? "It's okay. I need a ride and he has a decent car."

Nanette nodded dubiously and went to the front desk to buzz them out.

Bella waved as they left but had to jerk her hand back before Fane slammed it in the closing door. She whirled on him. "What did you do with the orb?"

"I left it with the Bookkeeper. He's trying to decide whether there's a message from Thorne tucked inside along with the demons."

"A message other than 'fuck you'?"

"That part seemed pretty clear." He crunched over the salt on the sidewalk as he headed for the Porsche. Bella trailed behind, staring down at her boots.

In the old days, salt was used as a defense against evil powers. The ability of salt to draw, purify and preserve on the corporeal plane had been extended to the metaphysical realm. Clothed in flesh, she felt nothing, but as an imp, she had avoided its sting. Did she dare rely on the protective power of potato chips?

She kicked a pebble of salt and watched it bounce across the pavement to hit Fane's boot. He had stopped at the Porsche and was waiting for her, blocking the passenger door.

She wrapped her arms around herself, her coat suddenly seeming far too thin against the iciness of his glare. "Are we going?"

"Why did you use Nanette to show the wickedness in the orb?"

"Because the talyan and I couldn't trigger that response." She met his cold eyes with her own searing glare. "And neither could you."

He pitched his voice low and intent. "The divine presence is still inside me."

Who was he trying to convince? If she hadn't been so miserable herself, she might have enjoyed mocking him. "Probably. But it's buried so deep, I couldn't get to it. Even when I tried."

"I want to end evil just as much as Nanette. Her husband was killed by djinn-men, but I—" He slammed his palm on the car roof.

When he didn't go on, Bella lifted her chin. "We all face demons. Some of us get to face them with angels inside. Some of us don't. But the orb didn't react to her desire to destroy it. It flinched from her love."

His hand on the Porsche fisted, and his fingernails squealed against the paint. "I have that too."

She curled her lips in a sneer. "You can't even say it."

He took a long step toward her and raised his hand.

Inadvertently, she turned her cheek, not that she thought he would hit her, but she *had* tried to punch him...

Instead, he laid his long fingers against her cold jaw and tilted her face up to his. His mouth—how did he stay so warm?—slanted over hers, his tongue tracing the seam of her lips with a power that left her gasping, opening to him.

He cupped his hand behind her head, sinking his fingers into her hair, and tilted her to his desire.

She closed her eyes and flattened her palms against his chest, giving in to the kiss, possessed by it, by him.

Finally, he lifted his head. "See?"

Slowly, she dragged her heavy lashes upward, knowing he would see the flash of cloudy gray cataracts. "I don't," she said. "So say it."

She waited for him to show her she was wrong, but he only yanked open the passenger door for her and stalked away.

Tucking herself into the smooth, cold leather as she waited for him to come around, she wondered why she wanted so badly to be wrong.

Chapter 8

Fane peeled the Porsche away from the sidewalk. All the baby Jesuses were gone, so why did he still feel like there were a few dozen accusing eyes staring into the back of his head?

Maybe that was just his angel.

Battles weren't won with love, he wanted to tell it. One birthday and two thousand years of history were still proving that.

He pedaled the gas, letting the buck of the engine distract him. This time of the morning, the empty street unrolled in front of him, asking nothing, wanting nothing.

Unlike certain other beings he might mention...

"Where are we going?"

And thus began the asking. "Home."

"You missed the exit for the Coil."

"My home," he clarified.

"No."

"I'm driving," he pointed out.

"This is a kidnapping."

"Right. Snatching someone else's body for your own use. What would you know about that?"

As he said it, he winced. That was cruel, even for him.

Bella didn't move a muscle, just stared out the window.

What did she see of the night with her imp eyes? Could it be worse than the heartbreak he'd known was out there, even before the angel had come to him?

He didn't want to remember those days. These nights were

hard enough. He gripped the steering wheel as if he could throttle down the memories even as he geared up the engine.

"My house has safeguards," he offered finally. "More focused than your artifacts. You'll be safe there."

"Why?"

"The sphericanum gives all its wardens—"

"I mean why are you giving me a place now?"

He clenched his jaw. "I wasn't about to leave you at the club without any protection."

"You did a Vegas-worthy impression of it when you started to drive away with all my Jesuses and without me."

"I intended to come back." He'd just been so shocked. And angry. At her for lying about what she was. And at himself, for lying with her.

So now that he did know what she was, how did he justify that last kiss?

He couldn't. There was no good reason on earth for that kiss.

"Listen," he started again. "I'm not the bad guy here."

"No, it's Thorne who wants to detonate tenebrae bombs on a bunch of vulnerable old people at Christmas…" She snapped her fingers. "Oh wait. You wanted to do that too, didn't you? To somehow turn the tables on him. If you aren't the bad guy and then you turn the tables, *you* become the bad guy."

Fane grimaced at the tortured logic. "I'm not going to argue about this with you."

"Because I'd win," she shot back.

"These are hard times for all of us—"

"Yeah, what was it you said? This season can be such a 'spiritually difficult' time for people like me who…" She tucked herself tight, clutching her arms close to her body as if she was remembering the flow of blood from her scars.

Fane swerved to the side of the road. Beyond the narrow

ribbon of park, the lake was an unrelieved blackness, like an invading force waiting behind the city walls. He grabbed Bella's chin and forced her to look at him. He didn't know what she saw, but he didn't want her picturing Mirabel's last Christmas night.

"That wasn't you," he reminded her. "You didn't hurt yourself."

"No," she said softly. "I was the one who hurt her."

He released her. "We all have our sins." Wasn't that exactly why he needed his abraxas? How could he make things right without it?

At least she was silent the rest of the way.

Some of the big homes in his neighborhood were dressed up for the holiday, tasteful swathes of twinkling lights punctuated by only the occasional reindeer, which was amusing since most of his neighbors were the conservative sorts who would shoot anything with a rack that impressive or call the exterminator if their holly bushes were nibbled by the real thing. No plastic, blinking nativity scenes though; that would be totally against HOA rules.

Behind the security fence—which he'd installed after being broken into by a certain stripper talya—his house was dark, without even a wreath on the front door. For an instant, he imagined all the baby Jesuses adorning his yard.

So wrong. He punched in the security code at the gate, and the wrought iron rolled aside. He steered the Porsche around the half-circle drive, pointing it toward the gate in the event a quicker-than-usual getaway was needed.

Bella swiveled to keep the house in view. "Will the sphericanum shields let me in?"

"No one else figured out what you are. I'm guessing the safeguards here will be equally clueless. I think you're one of a kind."

"It really is a wonderful life."

He waved away her sarcasm. "Great idea. You can watch holiday movies until we end Thorne. I think Nanette brought me all of them when she was still a ward in my sphere. She tried to use them to explain divine possession after my angel came to me." He shook his head and reached for his door.

Bella made a small sound of surprise. "Nanette taught you? I would have thought it was the other way around."

"The angel that came to me is more powerful, but she's had hers since she was a child. Mine came…later." He pushed out of the car and went around to open her door, but she was already out and walking toward his front door.

He followed, a little suspicious of her sudden willingness. But maybe she'd just accepted she had no other options. He knew the feeling.

She paused on the front step, and he reached around her to unlock the door. He flicked on the interior foyer light, and the crystal chandelier sent glitters of light across the marble tile and over their feet.

But she lingered a moment. "I'm not sure I feel anything."

"I should have brought the little bomb and cracked it open here. Not even the stink of sulfur would remain."

She tilted her head. "Couldn't we use that against all the tenebrae?"

He hesitated. "The sphericanum does. But there's a price."

She took a breath, as if she was about to ask more, but then she let it whistle out of her on a sigh. "Isn't there always?" She walked in, holding her coat tight around her.

He hadn't noticed before how chilly it was. He didn't spend much time in the house. He had his business to run—the cleaning company had been scheduling red wine removals since Thanksgiving—and the sphericanum to avoid and now the league and Thorne… All of which seemed much more welcoming in

75

some weird way than the big, empty house.

Except now Bella was here.

He went to the central wall unit to reactivate the external alarms and crank the heat.

"You're freezing. Let me get you something warm to drink." He held out one hand toward the hallway stretching back to the kitchen.

His guest drifted past him, still clutching her coat. Were the sphericanum safeguards somehow bothering her?

Down the hall, she trailed one fingertip along the picture frames. He turned his head to study the images since he couldn't remember what they were. They'd been included with the house. Did she see the black and white images, or since photographs would lack all meaning to an imp, were the squares little more than empty space?

As they crossed into the kitchen and he hit the light switch, she said, "I thought you were married."

He stumbled, though he knew the mahogany was glossy smooth. "What?"

"I thought you were married."

The words burned worse the second time. "Why would you think that?"

She waggled her left hand at him. "Duh."

Reflexively, his hand tightened into a fist, driving the edge of the gold band into his palm. "So you thought that and you still…"

"I figured if an angel-man was willing to leave some of his shine around my place when I needed it, I wasn't going to say no." She leaned her hip on the counter. God, she must know the pose made him think of that night. Of course, his head hadn't gone there a hundred times without any prompting whatsoever. "But there aren't any signs of a wife and family. No woman—even a stay-at-home wife—keeps hallway frames so dust free, which means you use your cleaning service. So maybe you're just like a priest, wedded to your holy war."

"Maybe not." His voice sounded hoarse to his own ear. "I was married once. She left."

Bella's jaw dropped. "She left you?"

"With a quickness." He turned away to open the cabinets and stared blindly within. Even when he was home, he didn't cook for himself, so he barely knew what he'd find. Tabasco, sugar, WD40... Ah, instant coffee. He grabbed the packets like a lifeline.

"What was her name?"

"Does it matter?" He filled two mugs with water and put them in the microwave.

"Presumably to her it does. And to you at one time. Now I'm wondering what kind of woman leaves an angel-man."

"I wasn't one then."

"Ah."

He punched the timer with more force than necessary, but he couldn't stop himself. "What is that supposed to mean?"

"It means 'Oh, I see'."

"You don't."

She pulled a face at him. "No need to remind me."

"Nobody saw, which is why our baby died."

For a long minute, only the molecules of the coffee, viciously pushed by the microwaves, moved in the room. Fane realized he was holding his breath, as Bella was too.

He let it out with an explosive burst just as the microwave dinged. He snatched open the door and grabbed the mugs, stupidly. Scalding coffee slopped over the backs of his fingers.

He hissed out a breath.

"Cyril..." She whisked to the freezer and triggered the door. Ice cubes rattled into her palm.

He fumed. She was a blind demon, never in his house before,

and she knew his kitchen better than he did.

She reached for his hands. "Where?"

"Everywhere." The note of despair in his own voice shocked him. "Never mind."

"Just…shut up." She pushed him onto one of the high stools tucked up under the counter and smoothed the ice over his knuckles, her thumb brushing his ring. "Not as bad as birnenston. You'll live."

Birnenston—the toxic ooze left behind by the tenebrae—burned like napalm, nasty, clinging and seeping ever deeper. Of course the thin coffee wasn't that bad. Except…why did the throbbing in his hands seem to be sinking through him, making its way to his heart?

He stared down at their joined hands, hers pale and slender, his big and flushing angry red where the coffee had spilled. "Her name was Nicole."

"That's a pretty name."

"Everyone called her Saint Nic."

"For putting up with you, no doubt."

"Maybe she had an angel in her, and I never knew. She had our angel—our child—and we didn't know…" He flexed his hands against the spreading ache. "We didn't know until too late about his heart defect. There's wasn't anything we could do. Except pray."

"If there wasn't anything you could do, why do you still feel responsible?"

"I don't." But he did, and lying about it didn't change anything, any more than staying up all night reading about hypoplastic left heart syndrome could change a diagnosis. "I don't blame myself for Max's death. I blame myself for not being able to make it right for Nicky afterward. We just couldn't make it right again. For weeks, she didn't speak, and when she finally did, she said she couldn't stand looking at me. Every time she looked at me, she thought of Max. She said she cried just so she wouldn't have to see me through the tears." He clenched his hands, and the ring seemed to hold the heat, still burning though the rest of him was ice. "No matter how hard I tried, I couldn't love her enough."

"Is that how it works?" Bella sounded genuinely curious, and somehow the fact she was a demon who wouldn't know any better made the question reasonable and soothed the raw edges of his wounds. "If we hope and pray enough, should we be able to save a life, save a love?"

"Yes," he said fiercely. "Otherwise, what does it matter? What does anything matter?"

"Don't ask me."

He reversed the clasp of their hands, so he was holding her. "Now do you see why I need to find my abraxas, why I have to defeat Thorne? This holy war is all I have left, and without it... It will all have been in vain. I couldn't love enough, but with the sword, I can kill enough."

She eased her hands out of his grip, and the loss shocked the breath from him. He hadn't realized how much he needed her touch.

"Cyril, that is so..." She framed his face with her soft hands. "...So fucked up. And, yes, I see."

A surge went through him, a shock from the chill of her fingers, but also a gentler swell that mediated the burn of his hands and the ice of her touch into a strange warmth centered in his chest.

She leaned down and kissed his forehead. "Poor angel-man. The sphericanum asked too much. Even the talyan with all their centuries of sin are not so broken."

"Don't pity me," he warned.

"The tenebrae don't feel pity. That is too close to mercy."

"I don't want that either."

She tilted her head, the red of her beehive a match to his hands, as if he'd reached into her fire and burned himself. "Then what do you want, angel-man? Don't make it a prayer, because those I can't answer."

"I want, for one night, to forget," he murmured. "I want you."

She straightened, doubt sketched into the furrow between her brows. "You want an imp?"

Why couldn't she be a good demon, happy with lies and his downfall into temptation? He took a breath—as shallow and empty as the house he'd inhabited alone for too many years—and met her gaze steadily. "I want someone who has looked into the darkness. And somehow lived."

Still she did not waver. "I did not *look* into that place, Cyril. I *am* the darkness."

"And still you fought your way out. *That* is what I want."

She stood there so long in a silence so deep he heard only the shush of his pulsing blood, keeping its own time. This was his twisted purgatory: to wait for a demon to give him one night of peace before the next battle.

Then she opened her arms.

He picked her up—her red boots and her big hair were the heaviest things about her—and carried her upstairs to his bedroom.

The master suite was as big and empty as the rest of the house. He didn't even turn on the light because he didn't want to see it. Instead, making his way by the dim glow from the chandelier in the foyer, he bore her directly to the bed and laid her in the middle of the indigo duvet.

While he unlaced her boots, she reached up to tug out the pillows, but the tight tuck defeated her. She laughed a little breathlessly. "You make your bed as tight as a chastity belt."

"Not me. My cleaning crew. I've told them to leave it alone."

"They want to make you happy." With a mighty heave, she wrenched the duvet and blanket back, revealing the stark sheets underneath. Against the white, the sight of her red in his bed made his eyes widen and his pulse pound.

Slowly, he stripped off his coat, ignoring the ache in his hands. "Now I want to make you happy."

She knelt in the bed facing him, but her expression was somber. "Forget happy, just make me come."

"You should fight for more."

"There is light in that, light enough to hold back the cold and dark."

"Enough," he murmured.

"For now." She reached out and hooked her finger through his third button, the one she had stopped at in her apartment a million years ago when she'd told him she was a demon. "Come here."

What did it say about him that he was faster on the buttons than she was? He stripped out of his shirt while kicking off his boots, but she held up one hand.

"Wait," she ordered. "I want to see."

He stood in front of her, hands clenched, blood raging. It seemed the house temperature control had soared with a vengeance. "What do you see?"

"A man. An angel…" She flopped back on the pillows, her legs coiled to one side. "Why does the angel need muscles like those?"

"The sword was heavy."

Her clouded gaze drifted downward. "I'm sure it is."

He didn't know what she saw, but he felt the response in his body, his erection surging to free itself from the unbuttoned fly of his trousers.

She gave him a smile of such wicked promise all his memories fled, and his scattered thoughts converged to here, now, her.

Enough, he reminded himself.

He knelt on the bed beside her and reached for her glasses. "May I?"

"Please." Despite her permission, her lashes drifted down in a shy flutter.

He eased off the cat's-eye frames and folded them on the bedside table. "Do they make a difference?"

"To the people who don't have to look me in the eye."

He leaned down, poised to kiss her. "What would they see?"

"Nothing." Her tone pitched to a minor key. "Nothing at all."

Though he longed to cover her mouth with his, he lifted his head instead. "Look at me."

Her lashes lifted to half mast, her clouded eyes dark in the shadows beneath. "What do you want?"

"I said already: you."

She opened her eyes wide, and he stared down.

Without the glasses in the way, the cataract-clouded pupils swallowed her eyes in the low light. He didn't see the demon, he didn't himself, he just saw her, now, here.

With a sigh, he closed the distance between them in a long, slow kiss.

For a moment, her mouth was tense under his, then she parted her lips on a moan and wrapped one arm around his neck, anchoring him to her. The kiss went on and on, tongues and teeth and the hot exchange of gasps fueling the epic caress.

Without parting, he fumbled at her shirt, but the little buttons down the front resisted his big fingers. Finally, he just yanked the last few off and shoved the striped fabric from her shoulders, banishing the thankfully front-clasp bra with it. She tugged at his trousers and boxers, and he shoved them away awkwardly between their tangled legs. She laughed into his mouth, and his heart pounded as if the extra breath had expanded his chest, as if she had made her way into his body with that one laugh.

While she was distracted, he unzipped her jeans and sank his hands into the gap at the waist, sweeping his fingers over the curve of her waist.

She squirmed. A ticklish demon? With her scooted up closer to his chest, he was able to skim the denim over her hips and ass and down her thighs. Refusing to let go of the kiss, he struggled blindly with the skinny jeans at her heels, and she finally kicked them off inside out and gone.

Naked, skin to skin, breath to breath… She arched up into him, her breasts soft and giving against the hard thud of his heart, the tight peaks of her nipples a tease. She traced her hands down his flanks and closed on his ass, fingers driving into his flesh, pulling him closer yet. He angled between her thighs, his cock thrusting toward her, seeking a different kind of possession…

He yanked his mouth free. "Fuck."

"Please," she moaned. "Yes."

"Can't. No condom." How could he have been so careless? Had he really believed he wouldn't find his way back to her?

She yanked on his hips, lifting her body toward him. "It doesn't matter. I'm a demon."

"You're more than that." He kissed her again, hard and fast.

She moaned against his mouth. "You're an angel-man. I trust you."

"That's sweet, but if you trust me, I can't betray that trust."

"Never mind then. Betray me."

"No."

She thumped her head back on the pillows in frustration. "I'm betting you don't sleep around, and I can't get pregnant."

"What makes you think that?"

"You're still wearing your ring."

"I mean why can't you get pregnant?"

She turned her face away, pressing her cheek into the pillow. "There is nothing to quicken. This is a body with no soul."

He touched her chin, easing her back to him. "*You* are its soul now."

She stared up at him, clouded eyes even wider than before.

Then she surged up against him. The surprising force of her knocked him backward, and for a heartbeat, he thought she would leave.

But instead, she pushed him over the rest of the way, her palms flattened across his chest as she straddled his thighs. "Angels say the damndest things."

She shimmied down the lengths of him, her fingertips trailing over his nipples, her mouth... She smiled at him.

"You first," she murmured.

And then—ah!—her mouth found the hard length of him. He couldn't stop the jerk of his hips as she closed her lips in a tight suction that brought blood surging toward the tip of his cock where her tongue swirled. He sprawled back on the pillows.

God, too bad he needed his angel to kill a djinn-man or he just might let her suck out his soul.

CHAPTER 9

Mirabel had blown a couple guys at the club for drugs. Bella had done it just once when she tricked the club owner—the trickery hadn't be that tricky, being second nature to a demon—into selling her the business. But this was the only time it had ever felt...right.

She curled her hands around Cyril's cock, her fingers and his flesh interlaced and somehow beautiful. This was something the imp could see in vivid detail, this atavistic surge of blood and hunger, a force beyond the merely mortal realm.

She wanted him so badly, wanted to milk the brightness from him, to coat her fingers and her tongue, to drown the old, bad memories with his desire for her.

He shuddered under her touch, his breath rough but his hands gentle on her head, guiding her down. He gasped as her mouth enclosed him.

Under her stroking tongue, she felt the rising rush in his flesh, and she quickened her pace. His grasp on her hair was a little less gentle and she wanted to laugh, but he pulled her down and his cock nudged the back of her throat. She took him, and he groaned her name, so she took him deeper yet.

His hips lifted from the bed and she gripped his shaft with one hand, his tight-strung balls with the other, pulling him in.

"I'm going to come," he warned.

She hummed her acquiescence and that was the end of him.

She choked, almost withdrew, then closed her eyes and took

him another inch. He spasmed again, his whole big body racked. The hot spurt filled her senses with musk and man and the faintest hint of honey.

She lifted her lips slowly, easing over each ribbed vein of his swollen flesh. He gasped and tightened his fingers in her hair another notch. She paused with her mouth just fitted over the tip of his cock and hummed again, gently. His arms fell limp to his sides.

She tucked herself up under his arm, her head pillowed on his shoulder. He laid one heavy arm over her waist and pulled her closer.

He kissed the top of her head. "Thank you."

"You're welcome."

"Sorry if I was rough. It's been awhile." He kissed her head again. "How do you manage to keep your hair up like this?"

"Evil magic." She reveled in the squeeze of his arm. "Also crazy hair gel and bobby pins galore."

He grunted. "More magic."

Abruptly, he rolled away, and she made a sound of protest. But he grabbed her hand and tugged her across the bed. "Come on."

"What? Where are we going?"

"Shower. Double showerheads. I've never used them. Speaking of magic."

"If you've never used them, how do you know?"

"My imagination just kicked in."

The white marble bathroom was as barren and unnecessarily big as the rest of the house. She spread her hands ahead of her to traverse the featureless space. "It's like a cold storage locker. You need to add a decorator to your cleaning service."

"I don't need anything. You brighten up the place just fine." He cranked on the shower and steam began to fill the room. "Now come here. I think I made a deal with a devil, and I want to pay."

Under the hot spray and his hotter hands, she tilted her head back while he banished the bobby pins from her hair and the stressed kinks from her shoulders. She might wish he could banish the demon too. Then there'd be nothing left for the tenebrae to hunt, nothing left at all. But for now, if she wanted to feel him, wanted this moment, she just had to live with what she was: a masquerading monster hiding in the light.

Enough, she reminded herself. He wanted to forget and so did she. Then his mouth found her secrets and she surrendered herself to this one night—however long it might be.

* * *

Thin winter sunlight pierced like a sword between the white curtains, and Bella rolled over with a groan. The formerly pristine sheets wafted up the scent of sex as she pulled a pillow over her head.

How long was the night? Not long enough apparently, although they had used every single moment of it.

But today would be the shortest day.

A hand slapped her ass, and she groaned again, burrowing deeper into the blankets.

"Rise and shine." The pillow was tugged back from her resisting fingers.

She glared at Fane through the curtain of her tangled hair. "You didn't just say that."

"I did."

"I should have sneaked out in the middle of the night."

"If you'd left, we wouldn't have—"

She yanked the covers back over her head.

"Fine. Peace offering."

The covers a little farther away tented, and she was about to goose whatever flesh he was sticking toward her, when the glorious perfume of coffee wafted between the sheets.

She sat up carefully, pushing back her hair, and reached for the cup Fane held toward her.

"Careful. It's hot."

She took the first rejuvenating sip. Now she felt almost human. Almost. "Cream and sugar. How did you know?"

"I've seen how you drink. You don't do half measure."

She huffed into the cup. "How are your hands?"

He showed her his knuckles, still red but not blistered. "The healing power of…" When she raised one brow, he finished, "…ice. Your eyes are like lake ice."

She took another sip to cover her sudden nervousness at his intent focus. He was sitting on the bed between her and her glasses on the side table. Between her and the door too. Not that she'd planned to run away in the middle of the night. No, she'd planned to wait until just about now…

He bounced up from the bed, and she grumbled at his early-morning verve. "Come on. The bacon is almost ready."

Well, she could wait to run away. She'd be able to run faster after a good breakfast.

"I'm afraid I couldn't find a few of the buttons from your shirt." He pulled a T-shirt and sweatshirt from his dresser drawers and tossed them toward her. "Sorry I don't have anything in red."

"I'll live." She took the opportunity to grab her glasses and slip them on. With coffee and glasses, certainly she could face the day.

He tilted his head. "Why do you always wear red?"

"It's one of the few colors I can see clearly." Of course the tenebrae favored red. Red for blood, rage, conflagration. But she didn't need to explain that part to him. He already knew.

"If you wore white, maybe you'd draw less attention from the demons."

She shook her head. "They aren't fooled. Also, you're not supposed to wear white in winter."

"Fashion advice from the woman with a beehive."

She touched the massed red ringlets that had taken over after their hot shower last night. "Not anymore."

"I like it curly and soft. It's… cherubic."

She gagged on her coffee. "Go flip the bacon."

After he left, she dressed quickly in his borrowed shirts and her jeans, once she turned them right-side out. The memory of the frantic coupling implied by the convoluted denim made her flush.

He'd said he wanted to forget, but she wasn't sure she could, not now…

And she only found one bobby pin, damn it, so she had to leave her hair down, but she tucked it ruthlessly behind her ears. So there.

She followed the perfume of bacon down the stairs. The house, white and echoing and bare of almost all emotion, was essentially invisible to her tenebrae senses so she trailed one hand down the banister lest she crash into something.

The curve of the stairs led to the office adjacent to the front door, and for a moment she stood there, disoriented. But a gleam of silver caught her gaze. She drifted toward the big wooden desk and skipped her fingers over the detritus of a working man: computer, printer, various stacks of papers, a cheap ballpoint pen (she would have thought better of him) with the clip broken off (she didn't doubt he had done that), and a silver photo frame.

To the tenebrae, the photo beckoned. Bella settled her fingers where her imp perception found the psychic imprints of many touches though the engraved silver hearts were scrupulously shining. She studied the image of the woman, not smiling, and the tiny infant in her arms. Here, white meant not innocence but hospital sterility, and the color of death was the pale, pale blue of the baby's skin.

The glass had been imperfectly cleaned, and a human fingerprint remained hovering over the child's cheek, leaving a smudge like tears; the glass, so thin, but the loss an impassable barrier.

With a soundless sigh, she returned the photo to its place.

Between his earthly cleaning service and his divine calling, Fane worked so hard to empty the world of its stains and sins. But he would never forget this.

She managed to find her way to the kitchen more by way of the bacon than her sketchy vision. Fane plunked a paper towel-wrapped English muffin loaded with the folds of an omelet in her one hand and slipped a travel mug of coffee into her other. "Half coffee, half sugar and cream, just as you like it. And you already have your boots. Good. Let's go."

She had her boots because she'd been planning to sneak away at the first opportunity. "Go? I have things to do today."

"No you don't. You were going to wall up in your club and hide from any tenebrae who came caroling."

"And drink." She wished that hadn't sounded quite so pathetic.

"It's my fault you have no artifacts to safeguard you."

She had no defenses at all… She curled the coffee mug into her chest, holding its warmth close. His fault, indeed.

"But I'll make it right." He gave her a fleeting grin that made her breath catch. "It's what I do."

Is this what Saint Nicole had faced? A man desperately trying to do the right thing, armed only with perfectly prepared coffee and that smile? No wonder the poor woman had left.

Even hell itself might not withstand him.

What chance had one lone demon?

CHAPTER 10

Like a warrior braving enemy armies, Fane marched through the crowd at the Christkindlmarket, leading Bella behind him. Clouds had thickened over Daley Plaza, seeming to come down almost to the top of the decorated evergreen towering over the Picasso sculpture, but the plummeting temperatures hadn't thinned the last-minute throng at the seasonal open market.

Bella tugged at him. "My hands are cold. I need a Glühwein."

He let her steer him toward one red-striped tent. Of course she'd see—and smell—that. The spicy scent of the mulled wine had already lured more than a few chilled shoppers who browsed with one hand around the boot-shaped commemorative mugs.

She ordered two and paid before he could pull out his wallet. "Danke," he said.

They stepped into a space between two tents to get out of the crowds and out of the wind. Bella raised her mug. "Fröhliche Weihnachten."

"Merry Christmas," he guessed.

"I can say it in most languages." She sipped her wine. "I used it as a chant to keep the tenebrae out."

"Is it only during this season you feel their presence?"

She shook her head. "They are always around. But most of the year, they find plenty of easy fodder at the Coil. My little issues are lost in the crowd. It's only now, when I can't help but think about…about what happened that they focus on me." She looked down at the mug of red wine clutched between her hands. "I must glow like a torch to the demons. Like Mirabel did."

Fane almost reached over to pull her into his arms, but out in the open, with their big coats and the hot wine in between them, the word 'demon' reverberating in his ears, he felt strangely frozen.

She shook her head again, more decisively this time, as if she hadn't needed any consolation anyway. "If you've brought me here to replace the Jesuses, forget it. The defenses are powered by the believers. I can't do it myself. You need a soul to have convictions."

He wondered if she realized her certainty she didn't have a soul was its own sort of conviction. But then, what did he know about souls? He was just a foot soldier in the war against darkness. Fighting for the light had given him no particular insights.

"Instead of stealing other people's beliefs, you can buy them."

She grimaced. "Not just any knickknack repels tenebrae. It has to be the focus of someone's hopes and dreams and..." She slanted a glance at him. "And love. That's why the baby Jesuses worked so well. Christmas trees too—the emotions children shower on a Christmas tree put all the lights and tinsel to shame—but obviously those are harder to sneak out of people's houses."

He coughed on his glow wine. "You tried that?"

"Just once. I ended up with a handful of pine needles and a backside full of buckshot."

"I can imagine." He really could, since he'd had his hands on that ass not so many hours ago... He banished the thought. "Well, I know we can find something here with the spirit of Christmas."

He ducked out the back end of the corridor between the tents and cut over to the farthest trailing vendors. There were fewer shoppers here at the edge, exposed to the street and the wind. One stall, enclosed in thick canvas on three sides, swayed a little in the cutting breeze and a tinkling music like wind chimes rose above the murmurings of the crowd behind them.

Fane stood to one side and waved Bella forward. She stepped into the small shelter with a small gasp.

The interior walls and the ceiling were hung with bright mercury glass ornaments. Simple balls and hearts, intricate doves and angels, fanciful birdhouses and nutcrackers, even a fine-spun dreamcatcher, and stars, stars, stars swayed from every surface.

Bella's gaze fixed not on the ornaments but on the little man hunched at the work bench with a blow torch, a multitude of glass canes, and a flowing white beard.

"There really is a Santa Claus," she murmured.

Fane nudged her forward. "Handmade, one of a kind, Old World artistry, made by Santa himself. These should keep the tenebrae away."

The old man glanced up, his blue eyes bright behind his little spectacles and his cheeks red from the cold. Or maybe from the Glühwein at his elbow in a mug substantially larger than the cute commemorative boot. "If you're looking for cheap crap, get out."

Bella slanted a dubious look at Fane

He shrugged. "Here's a man who obviously believes in the power of his creation."

The old man glowered. "I'm the only one who cares about the work anymore."

"Not the only one," Bella said softly. She drifted forward. "What are you making now?"

He straightened with an aggrieved noise to reveal the small sleigh between his burn-scarred hands. He'd spun out the glass ridiculously fine, the sleigh's tiny runners curled high in front, as if in expectation of a terrible snowstorm to be crossed, and hung with two tiny glass bells.

Bella reached out to nudge the little bell with her fingertip. The ring was almost inaudible, high and sweet. "The Snow Queen's sleigh."

The old man thrust out his chin so his beard bristled alarmingly. "Not Santa's?"

"No. It's empty."

He cackled, more demented gnome than jolly old elf. "I could sell you gifts to fill it."

"And eight reindeer." She smiled. "Nine if you have one with a red nose."

Fane tossed out his credit card, his attention fixed on Bella's grin. The sight of it—white and wide—made his chest throb. It had been so long…

"I have a finished one." The old man pointed toward the wall. "Not the same, of course."

"No," Bella said. "I'll take the one in your hand, if you don't mind."

"It's not quite done," he warned.

"It never is, is it?"

He cackled again.

As the old man wrapped up the purchases in tissue, he gave Bella a long, rambling lecture on how to pack the glass after every holiday. "For your lifetime," he bellowed suddenly. "Through your children's lifetime and your grandchildren's lifetime, these will last."

"I need them to last at least through the solstice," she told him.

"At least. Watch out. The edges can be sharp." The old man swung his Glühwein-glazed eyes to Fane. "You've been here before, haven't you? Years ago. I sold you a tree topper star. Gorgeous thing, gold edged cutouts so you could see the silvering inside. What happened to it?"

Fane shifted from one boot to the other. "I think my ex took it with her."

"Ah. Very sharp edges, that."

Fane grunted.

The old man grinned. "So I suppose you need another star."

With two shopping bags in hand and enough money swapped to keep the old man in glow wine through the next equinox, Fane led the way back through the crowds toward the parking garage.

Bella trailed behind him, letting him break the path, until they got to the relatively clear sidewalk where she sidled up beside him. "So you and Nicole did your Christmas shopping there."

"She said the mercury glass reminded her of her grandparents' tree, and she wanted a 'Baby's First Winter' ornament for them." He stared up at the sky where the clouds had descended more menacingly, shaving hours off the light of day. "We never used it. I don't know where that one went."

They stopped at a crosswalk as a mob of runners passed them. The runners were all dressed in gold and white, and many sported wings: fairy wings, feathered wings, bat wings. The race bibs around their necks said Angel Run. Some were clutching fake candles, some had boots of glow wine. They all giggled as they ran.

Bella clicked her tongue. "Crazy."

Fane lifted the shopping bags and his brows, and she inclined her head in wry acknowledgment.

Toward the tail end of the pack, a runner in a white tutu sprinkled with gold glitter cavorted with a long, slender wand topped with a gold star. From the star dangled a string, and at the end of the string danced a small cluster of rounded green leaves studded with white berries.

The runner paused beside them. "You're under the mistletoe!"

Bella blinked.

Fane leaned over and, very gently, matched his lips to hers.

It wasn't a long kiss—probably only one change of the traffic light; maybe two—but when he lifted his head, the angel runners were gone and only a sprinkle of gold glitter remained on the sidewalk.

Bella blinked again. "The bomb."

He drew back. "What?" While he'd been kissing her under the mistletoe and for some time thereafter, she'd been thinking about detonating demons. The heat curling thought his veins fizzled away.

The crosswalk sign blinked, and she started across, the clack of her heels a staccato counterpoint to her words. "The demons are trapped inside the orbs, right, at least until the glass is broken, and then we have a catastrophic eruption of churning tenebrae emanations. We can't move the orbs for fear of triggering them; we can't move the residents at the home for fear of the same. But, what if we were able to catch the tenebrae as they emerge?" She tapped the paper bag in his hand. "These ornaments made me think; the djinn-men aren't the only ones to blow glass. Instead of dreamcatchers, we'd have demoncatchers."

He paced alongside her. "I have no doubt the talyan are considering all the angles."

She scoffed. "You've seen the crap cars they drive. They don't have the resources for extreme demonic containment."

He frowned. "The league isn't interested in containment anyway. They're like me; they do crackdown, clear-out and cleanup."

She stared down at her boots, her shoulders hunched. "I'm thinking of another way."

"There's only one way to deal with—" He cut himself off, but she didn't look up. Of course she knew what he'd been about to say.

How had he forgotten, even for a moment, what she was?

But wasn't that exactly what he'd told her, he wanted to forget, just for a night? Yet the sun had risen—as much as a northern sun would rise, anyway—and here he was, still side by side with a demon in the stolen body of a dead girl.

She tucked her hands into opposite sleeves of her parka, the faux fur cuffs making a thick muff. "If we could just stop them where they can't hurt anyone, if they never had a chance to get at the old people or anyone else…"

If only she hadn't.

Her words remained as unsaid as his, but still the echo reverberated between them, pushing them a few steps apart as they walked.

"You're talking about more than a few really big glass ornaments," he said. "It'd need to withstand the earthly explosion of Thorne's gifts plus the supernatural forces inside. We'd need abraxas-strength power." His hand tightened around the rough twine handle of the shopping bags. Nothing like the smooth, flowing, living grace of his sword.

Bella glanced away. "Impossible, I guess."

As impossible as reclaiming his blesséd weapon. He knew she hadn't meant that; still, the implication was inescapable. And it cut deeper than demon glass or holy steel.

Finally, he said, "Only one place might give you what you want."

Since obviously that wasn't him.

* * *

Fane parked the Porsche across the street from the gleaming glass and steel office building he thought he'd never see again. He turned to Bella. "Here's the plan—"

Reflected lights from the building glinted in her glasses, dimmer and distorted. "We go inside sphericanum headquarters, introduce ourselves as an ex-warden and an imp, and get our heads chopped off."

He narrowed his eyes. "This is why I'll make the plans, thank you."

"The sphericanum isn't going to help us. You are a rebel now, as far as they are concerned, and I am anathema, or worse. I don't even know what's worse than that." She hunkered down in her seat, and the fluffy ruff of her coat puffed up around her nose, muffling her voice. "I've seen them shred tenebrae until there isn't even dust left to float away on the wind."

He wanted to reach for her, to soothe her fears. Instead, he drummed his fingers on the steering wheel. "The sphericanum has tricks we could use."

"We don't need them that badly."

"You don't place bombs before Christmas because you're going to be on vacation until after New Year's. Thorne will act sooner, not later." He stared up at the towering angelic command building. "Ending the djinn threat is a purpose that rises above sphere prejudice."

"There is no *above* the sphere," she reminded him. "There is only under. Preferably six feet under, as far as they're concerned. And their prejudice is *always* extreme prejudice. Hence the head chopping."

"If I can make them see reason—"

"Because zeal and reason go so well together. Like a bottle of Everclear and a blow torch."

He scowled. "You could give the Grinch lessons in gloom."

She'd taken out one of the glass baubles they'd bought at the Christkindlmarket when he'd first suggested their stop at the sphericanum headquarters, and now she clutched the little red and gold sphere like she wanted to crawl inside it herself. "I'm most likely going to be attacked by demons and sucked back into the tenebraeternum on the anniversary of my birth death. I really didn't want to speed up the process by walking into heaven central."

"It's better if you wait here anyway."

He slammed out of the car, but when he crossed the street she was only half a step behind him.

The front door was not guarded, although the security punch pad was an upscale model protected from the weather by a cover designed to look like a gate with a pearly finish. Somebody in the building had a sense of humor, but Fane had never met him or her.

He aimed his finger at the intercom button, then tried his code instead. The door lock clicked open.

Bella settled back on her heels. "Huh. Trusting."

"Or trap."

She sighed.

After the whimsy of the pearly gate, the lobby inside was uninspired Class A corporate. Fane marched them past the potted palms decorated with silver tinsel to the elevator.

As the door opened, Bella hesitated.

Fane took out his keys. "You can wait in the car."

She took the keys, running her fingertip over the ridges. He swallowed back the unexpected surge of disappointment that she was going to leave.

"Danke," she said, but then she walked into the elevator.

He followed and held out his hands for the keys. "I don't want a blind girl driving my Porsche."

"Don't be so sexist."

He entered his security code again and stabbed the top-floor button. "It's not the sex part I have trouble with."

She stared up at the ascending numbers. "So I noticed."

He sputtered, but she hiked up the hem of her parka and tucked the keys into the front pocket of her tight jeans. Clearly he wasn't getting those keys back unless he wanted to wrestle her down and rummage around in her pants. The thought had a certain charm, but was not recommended protocol in the elevator of an angelic stronghold. The speedy elevator arrived at their destination before he could come up with another plan.

So much for being the one with the plans.

The elevator doors opened and they faced five angelic wardens, all clad in white and barefoot, like something from a Christmas postcard.

All with weapons drawn.

CHAPTER 11

Bella pushed her glasses higher on her nose—a thin disguise, those two brittle panes of glass—and let out a shuddering breath. Maybe her last one if the wardens' massed surge of righteous fury was any indication.

Fane braced his hand in the closing elevator door. "I wouldn't have thought you'd be so careless as to leave my code active."

The warden in the middle angled a shepherd's crook across his chest. To the imp, the crook blazed, molten streams of etheric energy spiraling upward like ghostly fire. "We would not have thought you would be so stupid as to use it."

She heard herself say, "I suppose you both learned a lesson."

Wow, she so did not need that focused golden fuming—Fane included—upon her. She stepped past Fane's arm toward the wardens. If she was going to die, she might as well get it over with.

But the wardens retreated a step, except for the middle one. That was fine; she wasn't here for the VIP tour. She tilted her head toward Fane. "Back to your plan."

"Plan?" In contrast to his crook, the warden's tone dripped ice.

"To retrieve my sword," Fane said as he stepped into the room.

His slightly haughty emphasis on the last word made Bella wonder if the wardens' compared the size of their…weapons. Maybe a skinny pole with a hook on the end just wasn't considered as sexy as a long, thick sword. She resisted the urge to roll her eyes. Like the enmity wasn't thick enough.

But the warden didn't seem annoyed, or at least no more

annoyed than he'd been already. If anything, a note of glee lightened his voice when he said, "Your abraxas is irretrievably ruined. Even if you take it back from the djinn-man, its influence is forever poisoned."

Bella didn't need to see the flare of gold in Fane's eyes to sense his rage. "If Thorne's power has altered the sword, I will change it back."

The warden at one end of the line shook her head, her voice every bit as uncompromising, if less delighted. "The flaws will be permanent and impossible to absolve."

Bella coughed under her breath. So much for the forgiveness of sins. Maybe that only applied to animate objects. Of course, the wardens seemed unwilling to offer any absolution to Fane either.

She couldn't imagine—didn't *want* to imagine—what they would do to her.

Fane seemed to recognize the nowhere-fast nature of the conversation. "Regardless," he said. "Retrieving the abraxas from Thorne's possession will weaken him. That is in all our interests."

"But mostly yours," the male warden said snidely. "It matters little to us what weapons the tenebrae wield against us. We will fight on."

Fane gave an exasperated sigh. "But wouldn't it be better to just win one?"

"Corvus tried to end the war once and for all," the warden drawled. "And look where that got him."

Bella blinked in surprise at the tacit confession the sphericanum wasn't interested in ending anything. Corvus had wanted to bring the battle to a head, to force heaven and hell to at last confront each other without the intervening avatars of djinn-men, wardens and talyan. It had been almost noble; demented and doomed, not to mention devastating to the earthly realm, but strangely, sadly noble.

Not that she'd say as much aloud. No need to reveal her demonic origins so blatantly.

Fane crossed his arms over his chest. "Fine. Then consider your possible elevation through the spheres should we take out one of the most insidious djinn-men to emerge in centuries."

The warden hesitated, and Bella wondered how he didn't recognize temptation when it was right in front of him.

Of course, he didn't recognize an imp when it was right in front of him either. But Bella wasn't going to blame him for that; which made her more virtuous than a warden, apparently.

However, the female warden was shifting uncomfortably. Or maybe one of the glowing gold arrows in the quiver on her back was poking her in the ass. "We cannot consort with an exile."

Bella took another step up. "He doesn't need a consort, thanks anyway, but maybe you can work with me."

Again she quavered under the weight of those stares, but if they were going to make this happen… She dragged out the little glass ball she'd carried up in her pocket and balanced it in the center of her palm. "We need to capture and confine tenebrae emanations, and reversing the charge of the wards the sphericanum uses, we think we can—"

With the curve of his crook, the male warden slapped her hand.

The glass ball flew from her grasp and bounced once on the carpet but did not break. Bella gasped and reached down, but the warden smashed his bare foot down on the bauble.

Red glass and blood flared in the imp's vision.

"Whatever sphere secrets the traitor has revealed must go with you to your grave, woman," the warden said harshly. "Which will be sooner rather than later if you speak of this."

"Sooner even than that, probably," Bella muttered. She knelt to retrieve the broken ornament.

"In that case—" The warden raised his crook.

Fane punched him. One shot, right past the crook and straight to the stern, square jaw.

The warden went over backward, white robe flapping.

The female warden jumped to one side, an arrow instantly cocked in her bow, and the other wardens were bristling with their weapons a half-second later.

Fane shook out his hand. "We don't use our abraxas against the innocent."

"There are no innocents in the war between good and evil," the female warden reminded him. "Everyone takes a side."

"Not everyone," Fane said. He did not look over his shoulder, but Bella felt the intent aimed at her anyway.

The female warden rumbled angrily in her throat. "The ambivalent should be the first to die."

Bella picked the bloody shards of the ornament out of the carpet. "No doubt you'll get your wish." She rose as the male warden sat up, groaning. "Let's get out of here."

Fane nodded brusquely and recalled the elevator.

The female warden cocked her bow another notch tighter. "Don't come back here again, Fane. Once was stupid. Twice will be suicide. And you wouldn't want that stain on your soul, would you?"

He didn't reply, just faced the elevator doors until they opened and strode in.

Bella kept a wary eye on the golden glow of the enraged angels, but they made no further moves.

She and Fane descended in silence. She wondered if the descent felt more metaphorical to him, once again kicked out of his celestial standing. She cleared her throat. "That went well."

He stared at the dropping numbers. "We still have our heads."

"And angelic blood spoor. The divine essence can be used to bless artifacts used against the tenebrae. The reliquary I have at my apartment supposedly has a saint's knucklebone, but I'm pretty sure it's a pig's tail bone. Unless the saint cracked his knuckles a lot."

"You're babbling."

"I do that when I'm grateful to be alive."

The elevator door opened and they marched across the lobby, which was filled with wardens in white who parted slower than the Red Sea to let them pass.

Bella shivered at the threat of those golden glares—some mere sparks, some bright enough to scorch—and moved closer to Fane, but no one tried to stop them. Too bad, in a way. Certainly she'd be safe from the tenebrae here in sphericanum central.

Fane reached for the front door, but it opened before he touched it. An angelic possessed dressed in white overalls waved them out, grumbling, "They told me I have to replace the entire keypad."

"Sucks to be you," Bella said.

The lesser ward jerked his thumb toward Fane. "Not as much as it sucks to be him."

Fane ignored the other angelic possessed as he stalked past. He held his flattened palm out to Bella.

She put the broken ornament in his hand. "You're upset. I'll drive."

He glowered, first at the glass, then at her. "I'll be upset *if* you drive."

"Which will be a nice distraction for you. I'm so thoughtful that way." She pointed the fob at the Porsche and the headlights flashed a silvery halogen welcome through spits of icy rain.

She shivered again. Already the night threatened. Shadows seemed to decant from the low clouds, dripping down the sides of the tall buildings and spreading across the pavement toward her boots.

She opened the passenger door and then whisked around the front of the car.

Fane slapped his palms down on the roof. "I'm serious."

"So I've noticed. And I'm driving." She slid into the driver's seat and ran her hands over the controls, familiarizing herself with the touch of fine leather and chrome. Still, Fane didn't plunk himself down into the passenger seat until she actually started up the engine with a somewhat unnecessary roar.

He dumped the bloody glass shards into the center console coin holder. "I suppose it doesn't really matter if I die."

"That's the spirit." She peeled smoothly away from the curb.

His fingers clenched the arm rest. "You didn't even check your blindspot."

She looked at him. "Do you hear how silly you just sounded? I'm blind-ish, remember?"

He slumped lower yet. "Oh, how the mighty have fallen."

"Were you mighty?"

His hand spasmed again on the arm rest between them. For him, she realized, talking about his loss was more terrifying than handing over his keys.

"Not almighty," he said at last. "But mighty enough."

"And now?"

"Mighty pissed. They want to banish me, fine, but to refuse a chance to confront Thorne? Why else are we here?"

"I think their problem was not the confrontation but the company."

He snorted. "Shouldn't matter."

"Because the company you keep doesn't matter to you?" She kept her eyes forward, not sure what she wanted him to say. Did she want him to care about the company he kept? But then, if an angel-man had any sort of judgment, he wouldn't be with a demon…

He drummed his fingers restlessly, as if ticking through the various answers he might give. "I'm trying to do something here, for everyone's good." He sounded aggrieved.

Maybe because she was an entity of lesser evil, somehow that was not the response she wanted. She turned off at the next exit, jumping a couple lanes of traffic.

He shifted in his seat. "I thought we were going back to the house."

"Why would you think that when I'm driving?"

"Because my home is the best place for you to be."

She contemplated all her potential responses and decided two could play at his game of non-answers. "I can't see anything in your house. It's like living in a white bubble."

He scowled. "In a bubble, nothing can get to you, which I thought was what you wanted."

"Not *nothing*," she said. "Just not the tenebrae."

He waved one hand as if the distinction was of no interest to him. It should be, she thought grimly; without the protection of his abraxas and the sphericanum, he was almost as vulnerable as she was.

She parked the Porsche in the alley behind the Mortal Coil and tossed Fane the keys. Then she gathered her shopping bags and the broken ornament and let herself into the club.

Her heels tapped a slow, boring tempo down the back hall. So empty, so quiet. Sometimes she wished she kept the place hopping during the holidays, as a way to stay busy if nothing else. But she couldn't risk others when the tenebrae came creeping. She wouldn't let what happened to Mirabel happen to anyone else. At least not in front of her. Not again.

Despite her dismal thoughts, she found herself listening for the thud of harder footfalls as she rummaged behind the bar for a votive candle holder. But the only sound was the whisper of air through the ducts high overhead and the tinkle of glass as she dumped the broken ornament over the burned-down wax. She stifled her disappointment and turned toward the stairs to her apartment.

And let out an inadvertent shriek as she found herself nose to chest with Fane.

"I thought you were going home," she said.

"I thought you were going home with me," he countered. "Where are you going to hang your ornaments?"

"Upstairs. It's smaller, more defensible." Plus, she could see the pretty baubles from her bed and maybe sweeten her dreams.

He stepped out of her way. She hesitated a moment, but then with a mental shrug, she went up.

He was silent on the stairs behind her, almost eerily so for such a big man. Why did an angel need to be so sneaky? It had the power of goodness and light on its side.

But she felt the weight of his gaze, like the memory of his hand running down her naked back, and suddenly goodness and light seemed very far away.

She hurried a little faster up the stairs.

In her apartment, she hung her parka on the row of hooks by the door and kicked off her boots before taking the broken ornament to the reliquary. The antique was in the classic French style, like a miniature gilt-copper cathedral with rock crystal windows and a red enameled front door. With her fingernail, she popped the tiny latch and slid the candle into the depths.

"Watch out." Fane's hands on her shoulders made her start. "There's still broken glass on the floor from when you threw your drink." He guided her to one side then knelt to sweep up the trash.

She bit her lip. "You don't have to do that."

"If I cut myself, you can add it to your collection. Unless the blood from an outcast angel is useless."

"I guess it depends on how you cut yourself. The warden shed his blood to reject us, to repel what he saw as a transgression. That impulse works against the tenebrae." She ran her finger over the peaked steeples of the reliquary, and the copper spires thrummed an almost musical arpeggio. Did she dare ask if he would shed his blood for her? Or some other bodily fluid?

Her mouth felt swollen where she had nibbled at it, and when he stood up, looming over her, she couldn't help but lick her lips. As transparent as glass…

He turned and went to the kitchen where he found her trash can under the sink. The ring of plain broken glass in the bottom of the bin sounded like her silly fantasies shattering.

Which incensed her. An imp did not want dreams. An imp did not need fantasies. Her only plan had been to keep herself free of the tenebraeternum another year, but here she was, exposed to an angel-man, half embroiled in a fight against a djinn-man, and on the sphericanum's watch list, no doubt.

Doing her utmost to ignore Fane, she unwrapped her new sleigh and reindeer team from their tissues and hung them from the curtain rod at the window.

"You won't be able to pull the drapes," he warned.

"This time of year, I want all the light I can get." She fussed with the spacing until they were perfect, then stepped back. The window was only a square of black framing the storm clouds and encroaching night. But the meager light of the streetlight below glinted in the silvered bits of the mercury glass, and she saw not just the reflected glimmer but the time and talent and joy the old man had blown into the molten glass. Drunken curmudgeon he might have been, but his love shone in the ornaments.

She gave the lead red-nosed reindeer a gentle nudge to set him swaying and then reluctantly turned to face her visitor.

He'd taken off his coat and stood with his hip propped against her kitchen counter, looking long, lean and mean with a tumbler of clear liquid in his hand.

She pointed. "That's a pretty hefty drink for someone who's about to drive away."

"Who's leaving?"

She tapped the accusing finger against her lower lip. "Um, let's see…"

He drained the tumbler in one long swallow and then stalked across the room toward her.

She'd hung her protections against attack from the outside. Maybe she should have been looking within. She took a short step back.

He didn't stop until their thighs bumped. "Yes, let us see," he murmured.

He leaned down to kiss her, a slow kiss that coursed through her like the silver the old man had poured into the blown glass, so she felt as breathless and delicate, with a bright spark inside her. She wanted his hands around her curves, his mouth stoking the flames.

When he finally lifted his head, his smile was as slow and hot as the kiss.

She swallowed hard. "Liar. You had pure water in your glass."

"Then I must be drunk on something else."

"Exhaustion, maybe."

"Are you saying we should go to bed? I've been wanting to get a closer look at all those embroidered pillows."

She choked on nothing.

He took her hand and turned toward the bed, oh so conveniently right there.

She took one step before setting her stocking feet flat on the floor and tugging her hand free. "No."

"The kitchen counter again? If that's what you want."

"Where is this going, Cyril?"

He gestured one direction then the other. "The bed or the counter. Your choice. Unless you have another idea."

"I don't..."

He crossed his arms over his chest, tensing his broad shoulders. "Don't what?"

"I needed a light against the darkness. You wanted to forget for a night." She matched his crossed arms, hers lower over her belly where the ache of desire and denial centered. "What more is there?"

"Nothing more, not if you push me away." Against the severe lines of his winter-pale cheekbones, his eyes seemed bluer than ever.

For an instant, her breath caught in her throat. When had she begun to see him so clearly? The blue of his eyes—no matter how blue—should be nothing more than another shade of gray to the imp. Then her heartbeat resumed with a frantic thud.

How had she gotten so far from the isolation and barricades that had saved her? The longest night was here and her tenebrae brethren would be close behind. Mirabel had died, the windows of her soul forever dimmed rather than confront the demons. Bella would never let him face that, see *her* like that. All she would have was a clearer view of the horror and disgust in his heavenly blue eyes.

With a slow shake of her head, she backed away. She had been the death of a hopeless, helpless girl; she would not be the stain on an angel-man's soul.

From the lies all demons mastered, she dredged up a casual flick of her fingers. "It's been fun, Fane. But the season is almost over. *This* is definitely over. Thanks for the ornaments. Thanks for showing me...showing me it was wrong to steal." Wrong to steal the Jesuses. Wrong to steal a night of light from an angel-man.

Wrong to steal... No, she might have just *given away* her heart. She tilted her head and let her smile tilt toward sardonic. "You're obviously too good a man to be with the likes of me."

He blinked in surprise, and the blue of his eyes winked out for a second; a prelude of what she would lose. "Too good?" He dragged his hands through his hair, frustration in every line of his body. "Maybe you missed the part where I lost my abraxas and joined forces with the lesser of evils."

"I didn't miss anything. I took what I needed from you, just like the imp took from the dying girl."

His arms uncurled to hang slack at his sides. "What is that supposed to mean?"

She steeled herself. "I mean it's over."

He jerked once, as if he'd been struck. "You can't just push me away. There's something between us—"

"Yeah, the unfathomable abyss between angel and demon."

He cut her off with a slash of his hand. "This is something more. This is between you and me."

"There is no *us*, just two sides of an eternal war, where you are the warrior and I'm the enemy. You are a warden, Fane. Ex, maybe, but that light is in you still. I stole some of it, and thanks for that too. But the tenebraeternum would seize it all."

"Then take it." He closed the distance between them, towering over her. "It's yours."

Oh, how she *wanted*. The furious heat of him beckoned her touch, and the storm of torment in his blue eyes hollowed her out. Not with an imp's ugly hunger, but a desire purely hers to have him again, to give in to his belief they had a chance.

But the tenebrae couldn't believe, and no light would ever be enough.

He stared down at her. "Whatever you want. I'm yours."

She shrank away before her own longing betrayed her. And

him. "No. I don't—" Her throat tightened, as if trying to throttle her rejection. "Don't want that from you." Even she didn't believe the wavering lie.

He reached for her. "You say I'm still a warrior. You could be too. Fight, Bella. Fight for us."

In the instant before his embrace closed around her, she found the demon's voice. "I won't fight. And I don't want you."

"Don't do this," he warned. "Don't push me away."

"I am not some tragic woman you can win back with the power of your kiss. I am not a woman at all. I am tenebrae."

"I've fought my demons already. I can fight one more."

She let the double octaves rise, tearing past the ache in her throat. "I am not your demon."

He froze, his blue eyes bright. "Too bad. If you were, maybe I could turn you over to the sphericanum and reclaim my ward. Or I could ransom you to Thorne in return for my sword. I bet he'd love to find out how he could steal dead bodies for his lesser demons."

She held herself taut, though the taste of blood on the back of her tongue almost made her gag. "Probably not. I'm nothing, more trouble than I'm worth, really. But you of all people have seen that."

"Yeah. You opened my eyes." Still he lingered, his very presence burning through her resolve.

She reached down inside herself, seeking the imp's inherent viciousness and Mirabel's final rejection. And found nothing. Those shadows she'd hoarded so long were gone. All that remained was his demand that she fight.

Well, she could use that too.

She stood straighter. "This time it's your turn to walk away, Cyril. Leave me."

When he shook his head, the disheveled waves of his hair

glinted with a touch of gold. "I can't."

"Then I'll go." She took one step toward the door.

"Stop."

She did not face him.

He drew a ragged breath. "I won't make you leave your refuge here. I'll go. Put an artifact over the door behind me. Nothing will get in."

Nothing ever again. His retreating footsteps echoed inside her.

Wait, her heart cried from the place where her shadows had been. *I lied. Stay.* She bit her lips tight until the words died in her chest. The hours were spinning down to darkness, and she would not take him with her.

But as the colors around her faded and the door closed with a terrible click, she sank to the floor. Over the window, the Porsche's headlights gleamed once in a silver wash and were gone, but tears spattered her cheeks for a long time after, as cold and dark as ice.

CHAPTER 12

Fane wanted to send the Porsche screaming away from the Mortal Coil. How could she stand there—with the Christmas lights glinting in her red hair, her mouth bright from the bite of her teeth, the rumpled bed *right over there*—and ask him where "this" was going? And then tell him there was nothing between them?

His every muscle clenched with frustrated craving and outrage—*this* was where he was *going*, damn it—but he couldn't even get up to the speed limit. The sleeting rain left the roads slicked and dangerous as he crept through the industrial distinct. At least there was nothing to hit; the streets were empty.

Empty as the place behind his fury threatening to rise up and swallow him like some heretofore unidentified tenebrae.

The parking lot behind the @1 warehouse, however, was an anthill. An anthill of black-vested, jack-booted, violet-eyed, demon-ridden madmen. And madwomen. They paused as he rolled the Porsche to a stop just outside the cyclone fencing. Ecco leaned in the open gate, his fingers looped through the wire as if he contemplated slamming the gate on the car.

Fane slammed out of the door and stalked toward the big talya bastard. The league males might hate him—mostly on principle; the league's history of conflict with the sphericanum predated him by centuries—but there wasn't a man alive, demonically possessed or not, who would harm a Porsche. "I want in."

The talya rattled his gauntlets across the wire. "Door's always

115

open." But he didn't move out of the way.

"I'm going after Thorne."

Ecco glanced over his shoulder and shouted, "Niall, the golden boy here finally got his curly locks on straight."

The league leader was standing in the open loading bay, leaning over a large gutted grand piano serving as a table. He straightened with a frown and picked up his war hammer which had held down an oversized map. The paper scrolled inward, hiding its contents. Much like the league itself.

Fane bumped past Ecco and headed for the landing bay. The other talyan watched him pass, their violet irises signaling their aroused demons. This felt almost as condemning as his exit from the sphericanum.

Disdaining the stairs, he vaulted up into the landing bay. Though the big rolling door was wide open, the angle of the bay sheltered them from the worst of the wind and spattering rain.

"The sphericanum will want no part of this battle," Liam warned. He rested his hand on the scrolled paper as an errant breeze riffled its edges.

"The sphericanum wants no part of me."

"They'll forgive you. I'm fairly certain it's in their rule book."

Fane shook his head. "It's over." In his head, he heard Bella's bleak denunciation: *I don't want you.* "I lost my abraxas. Which I know you haven't forgotten because a shadow of my blood is still staining your lobby—by the way, you need to hire my cleaning service—from when my sucking chest wound spewed most of my pints courtesy of Thorne Halfmoon who used my fucking sword."

The corner of Liam's mouth quirked upward. "Maybe you should forgive him."

"Not a chance." Fane let out a breath. "The only chance I want now is to get my sword back. And then I will pledge it and myself to the league."

Liam's lips straightened as both eyebrows shot up. "The league doesn't need a warden. Not even an ex-warden."

"And it won't get one. You need fighters. I will be that."

The talya's Irish brogue thickened with disbelief. "Will you now?"

Fane let the gold flicker in his own eyes. "The fight is all I have left." He glanced over his shoulder where a couple of the talya males were standing by the Porsche with their hands on their hips. "That and a really sweet ride."

"Then you're definitely in."

"Do I have to trade my wool coat for black leather?"

"Ask the Bookkeeper how easy it is to get demon ichor out of tweed." The league leader centered the enormous hammer between his feet. "You know if you join us, the sphericanum truly won't take you back. The bad blood between us is thicker than birnenston and twice as corrosive."

"We all have our battles. I wouldn't be surprised if we meet again someday on common ground."

Liam inclined his shaggy head. "May that common ground run black with the ichor of our enemies."

"Amen," Fane murmured. He wondered if that was profane now he'd gone to the dark side. He found he really didn't care. "How can I help?"

The league leader gave him a crooked smile. "Besides handing over your car keys?" He beckoned to his mate, Jilly, who clomped over with authority although her big black boots put the bright blue spikes of her hair barely on the level with Liam's chin. "Show our new fighter the plan. I need to take care of some human resources issues. Or teshuva resources, I suppose. Otherwise there'll be grumbling about the angel."

Jilly gave an amused snort as Liam headed out toward the other talyan, the hammer balanced easily in his hand. "Never mind the grumbling. It's the silent shiv I'd worry about."

Fane helped her spread the map again. "You were one who spoke up for healing me when Nanette brought me here after my last shiving with Thorne."

She batted her hand as if he'd said thank you, which he hadn't. "I'm practical. We need bodies, as many as we can get. Plus, I'm still new around the league." Violet trickled into her pupils; a sign of her teshuva's power spreading through her. "Some of the guys remember times when the sphericanum hunted the talyan to the death, like any other demons."

"Maybe there was a time for a three-way war. But that time is not now." He flattened his palm on the paper. "So what can I do to make up for my less enlightened brothers and sisters?" He paused as he studied the map. "Wait. This isn't the nursing home."

"We might not have a three-way war, but we're still fighting on multiple fronts. The nursing home isn't the target, or not the only one." She curled back one page to reveal another map underneath. "We thought the nursing home was a test, Thorne messing with us, knowing we have a personal interest in the place."

Fane traced the bull's eyes on the map. "But it's not a test. It's a distraction."

She nodded. "That's what we're thinking. A distraction we can't ignore, not with Sera's father and Nanette there. But if we focus all our attention there—which we might have done if we, meaning you, hadn't found the bombs so early—what is Thorne up to elsewhere?"

"No good," he murmured.

"Exactly. Which is why we started looking for other traces." She touched one red circle on the map then three more. "Here are where we found djinni remains. And by remains, I mean mostly sulfur-scented dust and old bones. Thorne has killed several powerful djinn-men we know of, so he has to be making enemies of our enemies."

"And yet he is still not our friend."

"Not hardly. It seems he's consolidating power—terror is such a great leadership skill—among the rest."

Fane considered the arc of kills. "He's setting up a boundary."

"Apparently. Which puts his HQ somewhere in here." She spread her fingers wide over the map.

"That's a lot of ground."

"Which is why we're all going out tonight and tomorrow: last-minute Christmas shopping and recon."

His gaze drifted across the map, marking landmarks. "What about the tenebrae orbs at the nursing home?"

Jilly wrinkled her nose, making the small stud glitter. "We're splitting our forces. That attack is meant for us—whenever it goes off—and we won't leave them undefended. Sera and Archer are there now, of course, with a few others."

"My house has sphericanum shields built into it. Maybe your Bookkeeper can reverse engineer the protections for next time…"

Her expression softened into a wry grin as he trailed off. "Yeah, there's always a next time, isn't there?" Then even her smile faded. "Are you sure about this?"

He crossed his arms over his chest. "Why is everyone questioning my intentions lately?"

She lifted one brow. "Not sure who you mean by everyone, golden boy, but maybe we don't all have your easy access to faith."

He stared at her. "What the hell makes you think it was easy?"

She didn't drop her gaze. "We fight hard and, unlike us, you don't have a teshuva's eternal mission statement to keep you alive. Thorne could gut you again with your own sword, and we might not have enough of our abraxas shard to bring you back. Worse, it was Nanette's touch guiding the abraxas last time. Since her husband was killed, she hasn't been quite… Well, you could end up dead."

He straightened his shoulders. "The sphericanum is unyielding, no doubt, but the league doesn't appreciate how we...they have fought against evil through the ages without the benefit of superior strength and speed, enhanced senses, immortality, all the other advantages of the demonic—tenebrae and teshuva alike." He stared at her hard. "You call me golden boy, but I am not that soft. If I die, I'll die fighting. If not with the sphericanum, then with the league. And if not beside you, then alone. But I will fight."

After a long moment, she shrugged. "I've always been a sucker for hard-luck cases."

"Then let me borrow a sword and assign me to a team."

She nodded and pursed her lips, glancing over to where Liam was still addressing the other talyan. "Might be hard to get somebody to ride with the golden boy."

Fane gave her a tight smile and dangled his car keys. "I think I can find somebody."

* * *

In the end, he didn't have to let anyone else drive. There was a quick scramble among the talyan who didn't want to end up in the sad league sedans, and he found himself piloting three talyan, including Nim, formerly the Naughty Nymphette and now a demon-possessed warrior with her high-heeled combat boots kicked up on the dash of his Porsche.

He slanted a glance at her. "How is Mobi?"

She beamed at him. "You remember my snake? How fabulous."

"I still have nightmares about him crawling over the seats."

"That's so sweet." She ruffled the sheaf of papers she had with her. "And it's probably because you are such a good person that you got me as your navigator for tonight's adventures."

One of the talyan in back let out a strangled sound. Fane met their rolling eyeballs in the rearview mirror. He knew them by name—Gavril and Pitch—but nothing else about them. He shifted back to Nim. "Where is Jonah?"

Her smile upended into a scowl. "He's going in a different car to a different part of the city. We're having a thing."

Pitch leaned between the front seats. "I'm telling you, if you would just—"

"La la la." Nim held up the papers to block him. "An extra hundred years of existence has not improved your understanding of relationships."

The talya thumped back in his seat. "Ecco let me borrow his magazines." Gavril gave a disapproving sniff, and Pitch protested, "Not *those* magazines."

Fane shook his head. After his own run-ins with Nim's one-handed mate, he wasn't eager to repeat the experience, especially sans sword. "I would have thought the symballein bond meant you'd never have 'a thing.' Otherwise what's the point of finding someone whose broken soul perfectly matches yours?"

Nim thrust out her lower lip. "Oh, I still love him. I just might kill him before I tell him so again."

Not wanting to know more, Fane guided the Porsche out behind the stream of dark sedans. Spatters of ice in the rain made threatening stars on the windshield until the wipers swept them away.

Nim rattled her papers. "First stop, the old post office building. There was another fire last night. They're calling it a creosote build-up, but it burned a long time, so it could've been birnenston combustion."

"Maybe just a feralis nest," Gavril said. "Can't have been much birnenston if they managed to put it out at all."

"Let's hope it is just a lone feralis," Fane said. "Having Thorne holed up in a major landmark straddling the expressway could get...tricky."

Nim grinned. "Us talyan delight in tricky." She punched his shoulder. "That's you now, too."

"Don't let her touch you, man," Pitch said. "If Jonah smells her on you, he'll take off *your* arm."

Nim flipped him off over her shoulder. "I'll smack you too."

He puffed out a dismissive breath. "Save it for your symballein."

As Fane sped toward the post office, he wondered about the symballein bond. The Chicago league had only recently rediscovered the truth behind the ancient talya legend. The alignment of flawed souls had seemed an unbelievable notion, imagined by desperate men staring at an eternity—or until they were killed—of solitude.

When the sphericanum learned of the discovery, there'd been some quiet grumbling among wardens. How could the damned deserve such a bond? The sphericanum's official response: If the demon-ridden talyan had to cobble together the pieces of two shattered souls to make one undivided, that was nothing to envy.

And yet...

For no good reason, his mind's eye conjured up a vision of Bella sprawled on his white sheets, her hair in a red corona, reaching for him.

That was nothing holy. Quite the opposite.

And yet...

He was glad to see the Art Deco bulk of the old post office looming over the expressway. Better to fight than to think.

Nim looped her elbow over the back of the seat. "Remember, this is recon only. We are not to engage." She directed a schoolmarm glare at Fane. "Even if the sword is there. Okay?"

He gave her a steady look. "Don't make me lie to you."

She pinched the bridge of her nose. "God, you could so be one of us."

He cruised the darkened building and circled the long block before parking around the corner. The talyan griped about the extra walk.

"That's what happens when you drive a nice, memorable car," he said.

"There will be security cameras in the post office," Nim warned. "Our teshuva interfere with the electronics enough that they won't get a good picture of us. But you…"

Fane pulled a black ski mask and black nitrile gloves out of the center console.

She slapped his shoulder again. "Oh yeah, you could definitely be a talya."

They vaulted the chain link fence around the perimeter—Fane forced himself not to breathe hard and vowed to add an extra thirty minutes to his daily workout—and cased the building. Vandals and rats had been through before them, as well as the fire department who had put out last night's fire, but other than a lone malice that fled shrieking through a broken window, they found no tenebrae activity, not even a feralis snacking on the bones of unlucky rats. Or vandals.

They exited on the river side, and Fane stared across at the city. Against the black, glistening sky, the glass and steel spires of the city—lit from below—looked suddenly strange to him. Gorgeous and tough…and so vulnerable. Like someone else he knew…

Nim pulled out her cell phone and dialed. "Post office is empty." She paused, one hand on her canted hip. "Well, I know, and I love you too, but I'm not staying home just because— Seriously? Dude, I totally almost put you on your ass at practice the other day, with one hand tied behind my back. Metaphorically.

Maybe you should be the one who… Hold on, I have another call." She muttered as she switched over, "I don't know who he thinks…"

The other talyan's phones erupted in competing ring tones of classical and hip hop.

Fane's hackles rose at the urgent cacophony, as if the angel already knew.

"Kilbourne and Chicago." Nim's crisp tone was all business. "Got it."

Pitch consulted his phone. "We're probably fifteen minutes out."

"Ten," Fane said.

Nim grinned at him as she spoke to the talya on the other end. "We'll be there in eight. Wait for us."

They raced for the Porsche. Fane vowed to add forty five minutes to his workout.

The ice held them back but they cornered at Kilbourne nine minutes later.

Nim shook her head. "You let me down. I guess you need more time on the practice floor too. You and Jonah can make a date of it."

The Porsche was a silver shark among piranhas as the @1 sedans filed into the industrial area. A scrubby, empty lot spread away from them on one side. On the other side, the big, low buildings were all dark, and the parking lots slotted with tidy rows of delivery trucks, abandoned until after the holiday.

Liam paced through the sleeting rain as his league assembled. "No visual confirmation," he was saying to those already arrived and the talyan on their phones still incoming, "but heavy tenebrae activity. Birnenston accumulation, ichor sign, and lots o' rotten egg stench. Still, it's a huge place and we would've missed it if Bella hadn't found the stamp on one trigger housing."

Fane stilled. He'd left her safe in her apartment, surrounded by seasonal cheer to protect her against the unrepentant demons that wandered the longest night of the year. "She brought a tenebrae bomb back to the Mortal Coil?"

Liam held up one finger. "I'm calculating odds on we'll find Thorne, or at least his workshop where he assembled the tenebrae bombs. This is big, people, so let's be on it. When everyone is here, we go." He closed his phone and divided the present talyan into teams.

Fane took a step into the league leader's space. "Bella took a tenebrae bomb with her?"

Liam frowned at him. "No. She's at the nursing home. Archer said she showed up earlier today with some artifacts she thought would ward off the tenebrae when the bombs blow. But when she was setting them up, she noticed the manufacturing stamp. If we find Thorne's plans, we might be able to—"

Fane cut him off. "Bella can't be out tonight."

Nim, who'd come up behind, chortled. "Oh, you're another one of those dominant, controlling, maddening mates."

Fane froze, the icy rain sneaking down the back of his coat. Or at least that's what it felt like.

Dominant? Fine. Controlling? Maybe. Mad? He hadn't been before.

Mate?

"You don't understand," he snarled. "It's dangerous for her."

Nim crossed her arms over her chest. "Well, then what the hell are you doing here?"

Behind her, Fane focused on Jonah, stalking toward them across the slick asphalt, violet fires in his talya eyes.

What indeed?

Fane spun to face Liam. "She can't be alone."

"She's not alone," Liam pointed out. "Archer and Sera are

there. Nanette is there. Ecco is on that team, of course. There's—"

Fane straightened. "I'm not there."

The league leader shook his shaggy head. "But most likely, Thorne is here. And your abraxas."

For a heartbeat, he remembered the sword in his hands, burning golden with the force of the divine presence within him. In Thorne's hands, the sword would be dulled, polluted, dying, not to mention a terrible danger.

But the sword was not a woman, alive, breathing, in danger herself. And willing to give up her sanctuary to protect the old people from the tenebrae while protecting the tenebrae from the league.

The fiery sword—which he could not be a warden without—was not Bella, fiery in a different way, without whom he might be nothing at all.

He looked at Liam. "Permission to transfer to the B team."

Nim chuckled. "The dark side, you mean? You don't need to wait for an okay."

The league leader waved his hand. "Go. Don't believe she'll appreciate your interference though."

Fane raced for the Porsche. No, he didn't believe that. But he needed to be with her regardless. Needed it with a burning passion like the abraxas which had once gone through his chest. He loved a demon. And he'd never believed anything so clearly in his life.

CHAPTER 13

Bella hung the old reliquary from the light fixture over the front door—the last unshielded opening in the nursing home—and glanced with a frown toward the big picture window in the living room.

The sleigh and reindeer ornaments twinkled prettily in the reflected glow from the icicle lights hanging over the porch, but she didn't like the look of the real ice starting to form at the tips of the plastic icicles. She hadn't trusted the balding tires on her hatchback and so she'd taken a cab to the nursing home, but it was going to be a bitch finding a ride back to the Mortal Coil.

Back to her empty, exposed loft.

But she was not going to bring the tenebrae that stalked her here; she'd gone to too much effort to make sure any tenebrae would be repelled from the residents. The talyan would have no reason to destroy the starveling tenebrae emerging from the bombs.

Damn it, this was supposed to be a rebirth season. No one—not the old people, not a bruised and lonely bartender, not even a demon—should have to die.

Most of the residents had gone to bed for the night, but a few lingered, including Sera's father, in front of the TV with cups of dark cocoa afloat with soft white sugar-free marshmallow stars. Nanette moved among them, patting hands, tugging up blankets, adding more marshmallows.

One old woman reached for her sleeve. "It's Christmas, and no one has come to see me."

"It's not Christmas quite yet," Nanette said soothingly. "Be patient. They'll come."

And if no one ever came, as no one had come for Mirabel in her need, what would the angelic possessed say then? If Bella hadn't known better, she would have thought the angel-woman was completely oblivious to the demon-stuffed glass piñatas strewn around the grounds outside. Maybe a certain peace and calm came factory standard with the uploading of a divine entity.

Except that couldn't be right. Fane had no such tranquility. Just the thought of him set her nerves humming with lust and frustration. On the plus side, thinking of him kept the creeping knowledge of her oncoming tenebrae tormentors at bay.

She was an idiot. She should have used Fane's credit card to buy every bauble in the old man's tent. She should have lured the angel-man into her bed with every lie he wanted to hear and kept him there until dawn broke.

She should at least scurry into the activity room to hide out with the tenebrae-snuffing talyan and their pretty purple eyes. She was pretty sure Nanette had given them something stronger than cocoa.

But instead? She was going to head out into the icy night to confront her demons. This was her last Christmas in hiding. Either her fiendish cousins would finally finish her off or she would stand against them, once and for all. No blesséd babies, no glittering glass, no saint's knucklebone, no drink or drugs, nothing. Just her.

This was the downside of hanging around with repentant warriors and angelic possessed.

At least she still had Mirabel's box cutter.

If only she could have one cup of cocoa spiked with something… No, now she was just dithering. She opened the reliquary and lit the candle holding the shards of the ornament with the angelic warden's blood. The votive was a good one from the club and would burn most of the night. When she closed the reliquary, silver flickers lit the rock crystal windows from within like little stars.

Without a word to Nanette, she headed for the front door. She would buzz herself out. No need to answer anyone's questions. She couldn't explain anyway.

She triggered the door lock and reached for the handle before it latched again.

The door slammed open.

She had to jump back, and her heart stumbled worse than her feet.

Fane stood in the doorway, his eyes as bright as the reliquary, but instead of silver stars, he glowed like the golden sun.

She looked away, denying the heat that tried to melt her from the inside. She needed to stay hard, as hard as the ice outside. "I have to go."

"You're not going anywhere."

She slanted a glance behind her. Nanette had looked up from her rounds and was heading toward them. Bella hissed at him, "I have to go. Now. You know why."

"I'm not letting you put yourself in danger for no good reason."

Nanette joined them. "Mr. Fane. I heard you were with the other talyan tonight." Her glance shuttled between them. "Is something wrong?"

"No," Bella said.

"Yes," Fane shot back. He took an aggressive step forward to loom over Bella. "You're not going out there alone."

Nanette frowned at him. "Of course she wasn't." When Bella didn't answer, Nanette turned the frown on her. "It's not a good night to be out. The weather is atrocious. And the tenebrae, of course."

"Exactly." Bella finally looked at Fane. His furious gaze cut at her, hot and shattered as the glass in the reliquary. "Sometimes a bad reason is a good reason."

Nanette shook her head. "What is that supposed to mean?" She beckoned, and from the open doors of the activity room angled toward the lobby, Ecco emerged as if he'd been watching. "Ecco, tell Bella she should stay."

Bella groaned and shot an accusing look at Fane. "You're making this worse."

Ecco sauntered up. "Nanette says stay. Stay. Have a cup of cocoa. You wouldn't believe the marshmallows are sugar free." He held up his gauntleted fist, letting the razor studs shine. "See? I ate half the bag and no sugar shakes."

Bella dragged her gaze off the sharp edges to look at the talya. He crossed his arms, gauntlets bristling, and he was not smiling. He obviously had no intention of letting her walk out against Nanette's wishes.

She lifted her chin. She knew one way to make them let her go. Hell, they'd kick her out so fast maybe even the tenebrae couldn't catch her. Assuming the league didn't kill her outright. "You don't want me here," she told the big talya.

"Nanette says stay," he repeated.

"She doesn't want me here either."

Nanette sputtered. "That's not true. You came here to help. Of course we want you."

"Bella." Once again, the warning was back in Fane's voice.

But she wouldn't be stopped by threats, not from him, not from the tenebrae, not anymore. And all she had to do was let go of the fear and the lies. Inevitability was its own sort of peace.

She squared her shoulders and slipped off her glasses. "I am an imp."

Nanette recoiled. She must have heard the ring of truth. Ecco was slower, or more skeptical. He let his arms fall ready at his sides and took a step closer. As he glared into her eyes, his irises took on the violet glow of the teshuva within him, incisive and lethal.

Fane stepped between them. "No. It's not like that."

Bella sidestepped just as quickly, reaching for the door. "There's no way to whitewash a demon, Fane. Let me go."

"No one is going anywhere in this storm." Sera stalked into the lobby, Archer's menacing mass right on her heels filling up the rest of the small space. "Fane, I can't believe you made it here without killing yourself. What the hell is going on out here?"

Ecco pointed at Bella. "That is an imp."

Nanette pressed the back of her knuckles to her mouth, as if she might be sick. "It's impossible. She can't be tenebrae. I used to see the evil…"

"There's nothing evil to see," Fane growled. "She's trying to throw herself to the tenebrae as penance for past sins. Which I know you talyan are so fond of."

"It wasn't a little sin," Bella shot back. "I killed that girl."

Sera peered at her with an academic's curious eye. "An imp? Slow down while I catch up. I admit, I didn't read all the league guidebooks when I was interim Bookkeeper, but I thought lesser tenebrae weren't capable of sustaining a full possession for long."

"I guess you were wrong." Bella cut one hand across her middle, as if she flayed herself open for scrutiny. "I've been in this body for almost a decade, ever since I drove out the poor soul who was here first."

Fane put his hands on her shoulders, almost as heavy as her guilt. "There was no you before the imp took the soul's place."

She shrugged him off. "Doesn't matter. The other tenebrae will be coming for me, like they always do this time of year. Their presence could set off Thorne's bombs. And that would without question be my fault. So let me go."

Archer unleashed his weapon. The segmented axe flared open, wicked as Death's scythe, forcing them all back from the door. "No one is leaving. The raw emotions in this space could trigger the bombs without a single malice floating by."

Sera shook her head. "When the team at Thorne's headquarters hits, there's no way the bombs here will stay intact. Thorne will detonate just to retaliate. We have to be ready." Her violet-shot gaze circled them. "All of us," she emphasized.

Nanette nodded slowly. "You're right. We're all in this together." She gave Bella a tentative, wobbling smile.

Bella clutched her hands into fists. Pretty ineffective compared to a battle axe, but her fists were all she had, besides the box cutter. "You all are so... blind! You think the tenebraeternum is going to be impressed by your teamwork and acceptance and—"

"Love."

The reliquary hanging above them all flared. From the tiny crystal windows, prismatic sparkles marked the walls like angelic ichor.

She whirled on Fane. "What did you say?"

He hadn't gone more than a step away from her despite Archer's axe. "Isn't that what you were going to mock next? The power of love?"

She narrowed her eyes, as if she could constrict the sudden pounding of her heart at the sound of the word on his lips. "Yes. That won't get you anywhere." After what'd he'd been through, he should know. And yet he was looking at her with those clear blue eyes as if he'd forgotten the anguish.

Or forgiven.

"Maybe," he said softly, "we just haven't given it enough of a chance yet."

The silence between them ticked like a bomb.

After a moment, Ecco rubbed the back of his head. "What the hell are you two talking about?"

"Nothing," Bella snapped. "With you talyan here and the relics I left, you can hold the line against the tenebrae." She looked at Sera. "Sid had wished you could bring the verge here, to send the demons back to hell. I will be your walking verge. Send me away and the tenebrae will follow."

Archer shook his head slowly. "I don't know how empty you think you are, but you can't hold that many tenebrae."

Bella shivered. How did he know her emptiness? Could those bronze eyes wracked with violet streaks see so deep? She didn't think so. No one saw her.

Sera laid her hand on Archer's arm and didn't let go. "We don't send anyone alone against the darkness. Not anymore."

"That's all a demon is," Bella said bitterly. "Darkness."

Sera plastered her other hand wide across Archer's chest, as if he was her Exhibit A. "You forget who you are talking to."

"The teshuva repented," Bella reminded her. As if the talya needed reminding she'd been possessed by a repentant demon seeking its salvation.

Nanette clasped her hands in front of her. "And haven't *you* repented? Why else did you come to help us except you wanted to make amends?"

The question floated in front of Bella, a star in the storm, beyond her grasp. "As if saying makes it so."

Nanette shook her head. "Not saying. Believing. And behaving."

Ecco snorted. "Well, behaving is in the eye of the beholder..."

Fane barged past all of them and took Bella's elbow. "If you'll all excuse us a moment." He didn't wait for any response but dragged her out of the lobby toward the fish tank.

Bella tried to set her heels, but some of the old people were watching and she didn't want to cause a ruckus. Instead she hissed at him, "Let me go."

"You keep saying that, and I'll keep ignoring you."

Finally shielded behind the fish, she yanked her arm out of his grasp. She rubbed her elbow resentfully. "I don't know how you can call yourself a good guy."

"I don't." He boxed her in with the glass behind her. Against the pale glow of the water, his eyes were bright gold. "I'm just a man, Bella, who ended up with an angel. And you are a demon who got a second chance. What are you going to do with it?"

She averted her face. "What about everyone who didn't get a chance? Mirabel. Your son, Max… You and your wife."

She thought he would flinch, almost wanted him to, so she could slip away from him. But he didn't move.

He did close his eyes. "No, he didn't get a chance. We didn't get a chance, to know him, to watch him live. No chance. But we loved him so much anyway. I'll love him always." When he opened his eyes again, the gold was gone, just the bright blue she shouldn't be able to see, that pierced her heart. "Imagine what can happen when you do take a chance."

She stared at him, trying to make sense of his words as if he spoke something even more arcane than the ancient language of the sphericanum and the twisted tongue of the demons.

Slowly, he reached out to cup her cheek, his thumb smoothing over her temple where her glasses usually rested. "I would love you, if you take the chance."

A panicked breath caught in her chest, aching to escape. What answer it would take with it, she didn't know, couldn't guess. What did he see in her that she didn't see in herself?

"Cyril…" She reached up to echo his touch. The bristle of his unshaven chin against her palm felt too incredibly real, almost painful, as he leaned into her caress.

"They are coming."

The discordant cry from across the room jolted them together as Fane took a step closer to her. From the lobby and the activity room, the talyan's cell phones began to ring, scraps of a half dozen tunes jangling.

Sera's father stood at the big picture window, staring out into the night. "The damned devils are coming!"

CHAPTER 14

The sound of shattering glass barely reached Fane. It sounded no worse than a tumbler dropped in some distant kitchen, deserving nothing more than a half-hearted "Opa!" and a quick sweeping out.

Then the percussive blast of etheric emanations hit the picture window.

Nothing exploded, of course. Etheric emanations interacted only haphazardly with the worldly realm. But the ornaments Bella had hung over the window swayed wildly, the reindeer seeming to leap on their strings. Just as well the sleigh was empty or it would have spilled all its gifts.

Sera raced for her father's side, sliding on a pair of sunglasses as she went. "Dad... Pastor Littlejohn, it's all right. Sit down now. Everything is fine."

"The devils..." But the older man let her guide him to a chair. He glanced up. "Sera? What are you doing here?" He frowned and reached for her shades. "Is it a sunny day?"

She gentle diverted his hand. "I came to see you, Dad."

"It's Sunday. I have a sermon to write."

"He better make it a good one," Fane mumbled. He turned toward Bella.

The front door stood ajar and empty, with the reliquary above it blazing golden light.

She was gone. Fane bolted toward the door.

Ecco stepped into his path.

For all his momentum, Fane rebounded off the big talya's bulk, although he managed to avoid puncturing himself on the gauntlets. "Get the hell out of my way," he gasped.

Ecco blocked the door, his shoulders filling the frame. "I just let hell out. I'm not letting it back in."

"Bella isn't a demon. Not just a demon. No more so than you are."

The talya half closed his eyes, dimming the violet sheen of his teshuva. "Why do you think I let her out? Let her fight, golden boy, so she knows she can."

"Not alone," Fane shouted.

Ecco grinned and stepped aside. "Since you asked so nicely… If you need pointers on the proper care and feeding of sexy demons, come see me."

Fane shoved past him.

He almost went down on the icy steps. The scattering of salt added texture more than melting power. The tenebrae orb in the lighted manger was blown open like some obscene, oily, sharp-edged flower, and Bella stood over it in profile to him, a red pillar against the ice and glow of the Christmas lights. Her head was tipped back so her undone hair spilled down her stiff spine in wild curls tangled by the wind, but her face turned up toward the tenebrae was pale and still. In her hand, an extended box cutter gleamed. As if the tiny blade could have any effect against the tenebrae

The etheric emanations, which had been confined in the orbs, swirled around the nursing home in a half dozen separate waves of greasy black smoke shot through with sulfur-yellow lightning. The waves chased around the building, stretching toward one another. Their shrieks—only half heard but felt deep in his bones—escalated. When they met up, together they would be as big as a tsunami.

He thought he saw the familiar shapes of the animalistic malice and the more monstrous salambes resolving out of the smoke, but the silhouettes kept collapsing back into the chaos. It seemed the imprisonment in the orbs had permanently mashed the tenebrae subspecies together into something new and—wasn't that always the case?—worse, combining the destructive power of the salambes with the preternatural quickness of the malice.

He dashed toward Bella as the demonic swirl sped faster. The grass crunched beneath his feet, each ice-rimed blade like a tiny silver sword.

For an instant, he thought of his abraxas, somewhere across the city in Thorne's hands. But he might have another chance to confront the djinn-man someday and reclaim his sword; he would never have another chance with Bella.

He'd break off a thousand swords under his boots to get to her. "Wait!"

She turned and he halted in his tracks.

Even though the churning tenebrae cloud was behind her now, her eyes still reflected the pitch black and virulent yellow…

It wasn't a reflection.

He took a slow step forward. "Bella."

She opened her mouth and the wordless cry that emerged was pitched across multiple octaves, only one of them human. The tenebrae clouds slowed, as if their attention had been caught.

Shit. He didn't want the tenebraeternum focused on her. Not now, not ever.

In two steps, he closed the distance between them. He framed her face in his hands. Her skin was cold, so cold.

He stared hard into her eyes, searching past the demonic overlay, past the haze of cataracts, looking for the one he knew inside. "Don't let them in. Don't."

The box cutter slipped from her fingers and clinked on the icy grass. She wrapped her fingers around his wrists. Was she holding on to him, or about to push him away?

"You are not one of them," he said roughly. "You are Bella now. I wouldn't be here with you if I didn't believe that." But even as he spoke, he despaired. Once before his love had not been enough. What made him think this time was different? Ah, but now he had an ace in the hole: the divine presence in his soul. "The angel believes in you too," he added, urgency pounding through his veins. "You don't think an angel would lie, do you?"

"Cyril?" Her raw whisper was almost inaudible, and her hands clenched his tendons hard against bone so he *felt* the shrieking roar of the tenebrae reverberating between them. "Cyril. I…"

"Yes," he urged. "You. Not tenebrae."

"Both," she said raggedly. "I can't escape…"

He wanted to deny her words, call out her lie, but what if he was wrong? Could any of them hope to escape the unbearable power of the angels and demons at work in their lives?

For a moment, he wavered. His hands slipped, slicked from the tears trickling over her cheekbones.

The tenebrae waves spun faster around the building. Half the waves had coalesced, swallowing one another.

As they would all be swallowed?

His numb hands caught in the tangles of red hair over her shoulders, and she gasped.

The small, human noise broke through his paralysis. He would not let her go.

He plunged his hands into her hair, cupping the back of her head and tilting her face up to his. "If you can't escape," he said roughly, "then I'm going with you."

He brought his mouth down slanting over hers.

One hot mingled breath and two tangled tongues. The simple truth of longing. He pulled her close, leaving no room for error or lies or darkness.

She whimpered against his lips, then her hands linked at his nape, holding him fast.

He would gladly kiss her until the sun came up tomorrow, until the sun went down again forever. It wouldn't matter because he had her flame inside him now.

Her fingers drifted down his jaw, touched the corner of his mouth, and eased him back. "Cyril," she whispered. "I have to do this."

He raised his head to look at her. Her lake ice eyes—a thin disguise for the vibrant woman beneath—reflected his angelic gold back at him. "Then we do it together." He kissed her forehead.

She nodded against his lips, then turned within the circle of his arms to face the tenebrae waves.

Just one wave now, maggot-shaped and viscous as tar. Even bigger than a train he had feared, it poised like a suspended oil spill of evil. The sulfuric lightning had congealed, and the thick, snaking veins of yellow pulsed with a revolting, regurgitative rhythm. He did not want to see what it was about to discharge over the nursing home.

She shivered in his embrace.

"Banish it," he murmured. "You've done it before. Every year when it came for you."

"Never like this. And I had my artifacts."

"The artifacts worked because you believed." He leaned his cheek against her crown. "You don't need the knucklebones to believe in yourself."

He felt her shuddering breath as she craned her neck to look up at him. "Can I believe in you?"

He kissed her temple. "Always."

She took a step forward out of his sheltering arms. He wanted to grab her back, but instead he followed, lending his presence and his angel's light to her fight.

"There is nothing for you here," she shouted. "Until you choose to become something, you have no place here."

Fane rested his hands on her shoulders. "Did you just tell them to go away until they can be good?"

She nodded, and her hair whispered over his knuckles. "I think they'll really take heart from what I—"

The mega-maggot reared back, faster than any tenebrae he'd ever seen, and plunged toward them.

"Watch out!" cried a voice from the porch, echoed by, "Run!"

Like he needed that sort of help. He flung himself to one side, yanking Bella with him. They rolled across the breaking grass.

The tenebrae cluster struck the manger scene where they'd been standing. Plastic shards and sparks of electricity blasted in all directions.

He used the momentum of the roll to fling her upright. "Listen to the peanut gallery. Run."

"No." She whirled toward the tenebrae, one hand outstretched toward the darkness, the other toward the porch where the talyan had gathered. "No one will die tonight. Not even them. Second chances, you said so. Was that a lie?"

He gritted his teeth. "I meant—"

The tenebrae maggot emerged from the wreckage, doubled back on itself, and struck again.

Fane tossed Bella to one side, but stumbled on the slick grass. He went down to one knee with a curse, hearing her scream.

His fingers found the box cutter in the grass.

There was no way his angel could take the tenebrae mass. Maybe if he'd had his abraxas...

Bella flung herself over him, which he might have appreciated more if they weren't both about to die.

"No!" Her cry was one, lone octave, only human. "He is mine!

The place within is only for me."

Then she kissed him, and the darkness around them exploded with stars.

Chapter 15

Silence.

Was this death? Bella kept her eyes closed, not wanting to know. But the soft press of lips under hers and the mingling of breath—not to mention the cold soaking her jeans—tempted her to believe otherwise.

She listened, and—so softly at first—she heard the song.

"It came upon a midnight clear..."

Was it midnight already? On the longest night of the year. And here it ended. Hot kiss, icy ass, and the tenebrae swallowing all.

"That glorious song of old..."

Who was singing? Fane's shoulders flexed under her hands, and she found herself in his lap, protected from the cold earth.

He lifted his head and smiled at her. "Listen."

"...From angels bending near the earth, to touch their harps of gold..."

"I don't need a harp of gold," he murmured. "Or a flaming sword. I have you."

"You don't sing anyway," she said.

He shook his head. "You've just never heard me." He stood, easily lifting her.

As he rose, the tenebrae recoiled, lifting like a storm cloud, and he placed her on her feet with one more lingering kiss.

On the nursing home porch, the talyan and a dozen elders stood at the rail. Nanette had the reliquary in her hand, and golden light spilled across the lawn, impossibly brilliant.

Almost as vivid as the voices.

Sera led the carolers with her clear contralto. *"Silent night, holy night…"*

"I've seen her singing along with the pop tunes at the club," Bella said softly. "But I didn't realize…"

Fane pulled her close. "Archer told me one of her first encounters with the league was singing a wounded talya to his death."

"She got it from her father."

Pastor Littlejohn stood beside his daughter, his hand on her shoulder and his deep bass carrying. *"All is calm, all is bright…"*

Ecco stood with his gauntlets over his chest, his mouth set tight and forbidding. Which reminded Bella why they were here.

She angled her gaze to the tenebrae worm, coiling above, held in abeyance. Had she been this afraid, this twisting mess? Had she longed for so much and believed so little?

"Let it go," she whispered. "Can't you let it go?"

The worm hovered.

"Sleep in heavenly peace…"

With a roaring shrieking cry, the tenebrae attacked for the third time. The thick yellow veining at the fore peeled back, revealing a gaping maw. The funnel seemed to fall in unnaturally deep, deeper than the length of the worm. Far at the other end lay a sullen nothingness more unfathomable than even the darkest night.

Bella threw herself toward Fane and he caught her under the edge of his coat. He had the box cutter in hand which he slashed across his fingers.

She cried out at the pain she could almost feel herself.

He flung his hand outward in a spray of angelic blood. The tenebrae shrank back, but not quickly enough. The spatter of red and gold burned across the worm in ragged patches, tearing holes in the ether.

"Sleep in heavenly peace…"

"Or pieces," Fane said.

The worm tore apart without a sound. Dozens of salambe and a hundred malice fled into the night, escaping the light and sound. And love.

Bella clasped his cut hand between hers, closing it tight.

He tried to pull away. "I'm going to bleed all over you."

"You've done worse."

He stared at her, stricken, but she tugged him toward the porch. "Let's get this looked at before you bleed out."

He balked on the sidewalk, forcing her to turn to face him. "I never meant—"

"I don't mind your blood on me. That will wash off. It's your heart, beating with mine. It's your spirit, inside me. That I can't escape."

"Bella…"

"And I don't want to escape. I want to be here, with you. I want you, around me, in me. I mean that in the dirtiest way possible." She touched his cheek with her knuckles, careful not to bloody him. "And I mean that as an angel would say it."

Without ever glancing away, as if breaking eye contact might let her disappear, he brushed back her hair with his unbloodied hand. "Outcasts, both of us. Me from heaven, you from hell."

Maybe it was a symptom of how far she had yet to go to be good, but she was fiercely glad he'd been cast out. So he could find her. Maybe they didn't have the symballein bond of the soul-shattered talyan, but their wounds—and their healing—made them right for each other. "It's like we were meant to be."

"Together." He didn't smile back, his gaze so intense she thought the blue of his eyes might melt the ice. Like she was melting.

She closed her eyes and tilted up onto her toes to kiss him. A gentle touch, cool as tears, brushed her cheeks, but she wasn't crying. She was happy.

She glanced up to see the snow sifting down. The low clouds reflected back the lights of the city in washes of silver and gold. With only the lightest breath of wind to tease them, the snowflakes wafted in lazy spirals, each finding its own unique path from heaven to earth.

Fane laughed, sending the nearest snowflakes dancing. He kissed Bella and sang softly over her lips, *"I'm dreaming of a white Christmas..."*

She blinked at his pure tenor, and his grin turned smug.

"I'm dreaming of Christmas with you." He tucked her under his arm, and they walked up the sidewalk toward the talyan and the old people under a snowy winter sky.

Ecco crossed his gauntleted arms over his chest as they approached. "Had a call from the boss. They found Thorne workshop at the industrial site, but he wasn't there. Just a bunch more bombs—most of them not even finished—and a note saying 'Don't Open 'Til Christmas.' And you just let all those tenebrae escape without sending even one back to hell. Tonight was a total bust."

"Actually," Bella said as they pushed by him. "This is going to be my best Christmas ever. Peace on earth and all that."

Fane kissed her temple. "At least for tonight."

EPILOGUE

Fane leaned back on the pillows of the big, red bed and sighed. He should have guessed grandma pillows rescued from yard sales would be cozy, especially with sayings like:

Now I lay me down to sleep
I pray the Lord my soul to keep
May angels watch me through the night
And wake me with the morning light.

He thought, as prayers went, that one he could follow.

Bella bounced on his chest. "Seriously, I can't believe you haven't seen *The Nightmare Before Christmas*! It's one of the greatest Christmas movies of all time."

"It has monsters in it."

She stared down at him. "Yeah, and?"

He sighed again, just to watch her bounce some more. "Fine. You get to pick the Christmas Eve movie, but I get to pick what we do after."

She traced her finger down his sternum. "Sounds like a win-win."

After the carry-out Chinese dinner and movie—which he admitted was pretty great, especially the music—she hustled him back to the bed. They'd brought up a bunch of votive candles from the bar below, and the lights danced as they sprawled across the mattress.

"Now for dessert." She tipped him over backwards and undid the button on his jeans.

He let her, then caught her hands. "Wait. I have something for you."

"That's what I'm trying to get to."

"I have something *else* for you." He snaked his hand under the pillow and presented the small ribboned box centered on his palm.

Bella sat back on her heels, a small line between her brows. "We're going to do gifts now? Aren't gifts for Christmas morning?"

"We'll make our own traditions," he said. "Besides, it's almost midnight."

She pursed her lips, then hopped up and went to the chest underneath the window. The framed square of night was frosted at the corners, a lovely frame for the snowflakes falling on the other side, a perfect backdrop for his even more lovely flame, Bella.

She returned to kneel on the bed, a wrapped box about as big as his shoe in her lap.

They stared at each other a moment. "You first," they said at the same time.

Bella smiled. "Ladies first." She handed over her box.

He started to admire the foil wrapping, but she made an impatient noise, so he tore past the paper. The box inside was plain.

She nibbled her lip. "It was sort of a last-minute thing, obviously. The old guy at the Christkindlmarket knew a guy…"

Fane opened the box and stared down. He whistled. "Snazzy."

"This guy does custom glass too. A little different, obviously."

Fane lifted the sunglasses out of the box. "Purple tint on the lenses. The talyan will be jealous. Nice."

"Shatterproof glass, of course, and glare-proof—which I think will be useful if you're working with the league—and a lifetime warranty on the black iridium frames." She smiled, almost shyly. "I had them inscribed…"

He unfolded the sunglasses. Along the inside of the temple piece, etched in gold, it said: *Welcome to the dark side. Love, Bella.*

He traced his fingertip over her name, feeling the slight serration, sharp and bright. "Perfect. I love it."

She let out a breath, as if she'd been nervous about his response. "I talked to the guy a little bit, about polarizing and half-silvering and polycrystalline diamond coating, and I was thinking… What if there were glasses to let people see etheric emanations?"

Fane slid on the shades. "If people could see tenebrae, they would freak out. Which would be bad since there's little the tenebrae like more than a good freak-out."

"But if people could see the demons, maybe they would know why sometimes the world seems so dark." She looked down at her clasped hands. "Mirabel would have known she was being stalked, and maybe she would have been able to fight back."

He pushed the shades to the top of his head. "Maybe you're right. You should bring it up with the talyan. If ever there was a league willing to try something new, it's them. They took me in. But let's save that for the new year."

She nodded. "My turn?"

He handed over the box, swallowing down the sudden acceleration of his heartbeat. "I hope you… Like you said, it was sort of last minute…"

She untangled the wide ribbon nearly obscuring the box and ran her fingertip over the velvety exterior. She angled a glance at him. "Cyril…"

His pulse shot back toward critical. "Open it."

She flipped back the lid and gasped.

"It's not a diamond or anything," he said hurriedly.

"I wouldn't be able to see a diamond." She lifted the ring from the box. "This I can see."

The ruby glimmered in the candlelight, dancing with its own inner flame. He took the ring from her and slipped it over the middle finger of her left hand.

Not the ring finger. Not yet. But close.

She held out her hand to admire the twinkle. "It's beautiful."

"It's a reminder. Every ruby has flaws in its heart. That's how we know it's real."

Her lips quirked. "You're saying I'm flawed."

"And real. And I'm hoping you'll forgive me—and love me—for being the same."

She leaned forward to kiss him. "Demon and angel."

"And to all a good night." He kissed her back. "Merry Christmas."

"Merry Christmas," she whispered.

And so it was.

Glossary of Terms

abraxas: An angelic-possessed's blessed weapon.

ahāzum: A gathering of djinn; forbidden since the First Battle.

ascendant: The rise of a demon within a possessed human; refers to the initial incident of possession and subsequent risings.

birnenston: Also, brimstone. A sulfuric compound leached from some demonic emanations interacting with the human realm.

desolator numinis: "Soul cleaver"; a demonic weapon.

djinni: djinn (pl.): Upper echelon of demonkind; fallen angels who are content to stay fallen.

djinn-man: A human possessed by a djinni.

ether: The elemental energy of spiritual and demonic emanations.

feralis: ferales (pl.): Lesser demonic emanation encased in a physical shell of mutated human-realm material. Physically strong, but not so impressive in the brains department.

heshuka: The unknown darkness; from Aramaic.

horde-tenebrae: Blanket term for lesser demonic emanations, including malice, ferales, and salambes. Also, tenebrae.

ichor: A physical by-product of demonic emanations not compatible with the human realm.

league: Isolated clusters of possessed fighters assigned to high-density human-population areas with the mission of reducing demonic activity.

malice: Incorporeal lesser emanation from the demon realm, typically small and animalistic in shape with protohuman intelligence.

mated-talyan bond: The synergistic combination of male and female possessed powers.

reven: The permanent visible epidermal mark left by an ascended demon.

salambe: Highly emanating demonic form from the same subspecies as malice.

solvo: A chemical version of the *desolator numinis*; produces opiatelike effects in humans while splitting off the soul.

sphericanum: The realm of angels, separated from the human realm by the gates of heaven. Also used in reference to the ruling body of angelic powers.

symballein: A token, such as an engraved metal disk, that is broken into two pieces and used to establish identity when reunited; from Greek.

talya: talyan (pl.): 1. Sacrificial lamb; a young man (Aramaic). 2. A human, typically male, possessed by a repentant demon.

tenebrae: Blanket term for lesser demonic emanations, including malice, ferales, and salambes. Also, horde-tenebrae.

tenebraeternum: The demon realm, separated from the human realm by the Veil.

teshuva: A repentant demon seeking to return to a state of grace.

Veil: An etheric barrier between the human and demon realms; composed of captured souls.

ALSO BY JESSA SLADE

Novels of the Marked Souls

The Darkest Night, Marked Souls #4.5

Darkness Undone, Marked Souls #4

Vowed in Shadows, Marked Souls #3

Forged of Shadows, Marked Souls #2

Seduced by Shadows, Marked Souls #1

Novels of the Steel Born

Dark Prince's Desire, Steel Born #4

Mated By Moonlight, Steel Born #3

A Little Night Muse, Steel Born #2

Dark Hunter's Touch, Steel Born #1

Other stories from Jessa Slade

"Enslaved By Starlight" (in *Hotter on the Edge*)

"Prince of Passion" (in *Hotter on the Edge 2*)

ABOUT THE AUTHOR

Although a grade-school aptitude test predicted Jessa Slade would someday become a farmer, her fate as a writer was sealed when she won a writing contest where the prize was any book she wanted. Any book! Can you imagine? Since then, her imagination has taken her into paranormal romance, urban fantasy romance, and award-winning science fiction romance—basically, anything with woo-woo and woo-hoo! She loves to hear from readers and can be found at all the usual online haunts as Jessa Slade on Goodreads, Facebook, Twitter, and Pinterest. Her latest book news and newsletter mailing list are on her website at www.JessaSlade.com.